RIVER AND STONE

MORGANTOWN WRITERS GROUP

RIVER AND STONE

ANTHOLOGY OF SHORT STORIES

Edited by Melissa Reynolds

CONTENTS

George M. Lies

Founder Morgantown Writers Group 1994-2024

Dedication By Erica Lies

Over the course of his life, George Marshall Lies was known by many names, but I'm the only person whoever called him "dad." If you knew him at all, you won't be surprised to hear he wasn't a conventional father. He didn't fix things or tune up my car. He's never touched a barbeque. And he sure as hell never coached little league.

Instead, he taught me how to be an artist. From the time I was a toddler, he instilled creativity into everything. Some of my earliest memories are making a dollhouse out of shoeboxes, which we painted and colored with crayons. All so my collection of Smurfs would have a place to live.

Unsurprisingly, a good chunk of my childhood was spent behind writers' conference tables and (perhaps scandalously) inside his favorite bar where I ate pretzel sticks and drank Shirley Temples. Before the age of ten, he had taught me how books were bound, the different weights of paper, and the varying costs of 1-, 2-, and 3-color process printing.

Throughout my life, I've had maybe two writing teachers who mattered, and my dad was the first. I learned more from him than any college writing class. He taught me how to line edit, how to write concisely and clearly, and why rhythm is just as important as the words I use. He taught me how to have panache, and without him, I would have no style.

But I am hardly alone in having benefited from his expertise, because if my dad had a church, it was a roomful of writers. Among them, he will be remembered as a gregarious organizer who supported others and always had a smile and an insatiable appetite for culture of all kinds. He'll be recalled as a selfless encourager. Someone who did more for others' careers than his own. Someone who brought people together. Someone who brought cultures together. He's being mourned on four continents, which is a legacy unto itself.

Any writer knows that in creating a character, it's the specifics that make them sing. So here's a few of my dad's... He wrote me notes and poems on bar napkins. I could mostly read them. He loved Good & Plenty candy, orange jelly slices (the cheap kind), and pork rinds. He loved a good story—especially when he was telling it.

I'm not sure how to accept that he'll never mail me another scribbled bar napkin or acheesy singing birthday card. Who will I go to now for advice I will then stubbornly refuse to take? Truthfully, I don't know how to conceive of the world without him in it. But I do know this: He lives in all of us. He lives in me. Every line I write, every turn of phrase I conjure, there is a trace of him. I can only hope that he will haunt me. And give me notes.

INTRODUCTION

T he Morgantown Writers Group is pleased to present the anthology *River and Stone* in honor of George Lies, its founding member and leader from 1994 to 2024. The Morgantown Writers Group is a literary arts group that is part of the Morgantown Arts Collaborative. Founded in January 1994, at the request of the Morgantown Public Library, approximately 680 writers have participated in the group's literary activities over the years.

Many Morgantown Writers Group authors have been published or recognized through writing awards, both nationally and in the West Virginia Writers, Inc.'s annual spring writers' competition. Numerous award-winning and published works began as draft manuscripts first reviewed by the Morgantown Writers Group at critique workshops.

George Lies initiated the *River and Stone* anthology. Many of the stories within these pages were submitted to the Morgantown Writers Group's biannual contests. George admired the stories from these contests and wanted to publish them, so he brought in a new editor, Melissa Reynolds. When George passed away in April 2024, Melissa took over and opened submissions to all authors wishing to honor George and his impact on their writing.

We extend our deepest gratitude to the past and present participants of the Morgantown Writers Group for contributing their short stories to this anthology. We appreciate Patricia Hopper Patteson and Melissa Reynolds for their editorial work, and Iva Reynolds for her consultant with graphic design. We also thank our first readers, Edwina Pendarvis, Eric Casdorph, Matthew Smallwood, and Adam Horne, for their valuable insights. We extend our appreciation to *The Metaworker Literary*

Magazine editors, Elena Perez and Cerid Jones, for their expert feedback. Finally, we gratefully acknowledge the Morgantown Public Library for their gracious support in providing their facility for group meetings. We are proud to showcase our collective work and express our gratitude for George's imprint on and support of our talent.

MOUNTAIN STREAMS

RIVER AND STONE

By Melissa Reynolds

I have been struck through and through. How or when, I know not. Stairs, benches, and amphitheater all blur and fade. Time slips around me as I am held, suspended in ecstasy then terror and pain, joy and sorrow.

Echoes of myself through the years have felt this very moment and somehow line up to collide within me. I am the same yet different. I am connected to the past versions of myself, as though I am a worm that loops around, and some great arrow has pierced through all the different sections to pin me to some hard truth I cannot identify. I am young and old. I am virgin, mother, crone, all in one, all at once and the pain of each bleed into who I am in this moment.

Eight-year-old me wails, her knee scraped in a spectacular bike crash. Fourteen raises her eyes from the flame of a candle. Nineteen, dressed in a wedding gown, pauses at the church entryway. Twenty-two cradles an infant boy for the first time and smiles. Twenty-five suckles twin girls with dark circles under her eyes. Twenty-seven panics over a six-week-old baby girl, pale, fingernails blue. Thirty-one squares her shoulders, takes off her wedding ring, and lifts the weights. Thirty-eight turns her tassel and pauses for a photo as she accepts her master's degree. Forty-five types the last word of her novel. Fifty-two strolls the art gallery where her girls' art hangs, pausing to accept a glass of champagne. Fifty-eight holds her granddaughter and coos. Sixty-three drinks tea on the front porch and watches fireflies emerge. And somewhere at some age, seventy-eight or maybe eighty-eight, pauses before her last breath and blindly reaches out to eight.

Disconnect from reality is bittersweet and leaves me frozen. This always has been, and I fear, will always be.

Nevertheless, the Monongahela River flows by me—soft, constant, wearing away the banks and stones that mourn the smoothing. I sit on the stairs of Hazel Ruby McQuain park, forearms draped across my knees, and turn a stone over in my hand. I have sat beside many rivers and streams. Some rush and tumble, roaring at the stone teeth ripping through, only to crash over waterfalls, others are barely more than a trickle. I have swum in the swift currents, and I have waded in calm shallows. I have picked my way across slime-slick rocks, ice cold, and sank my toes into soft mud. This river is not so wild. The dam keeps it even, the bridge nearby spans it effortlessly, and the traffic places a bridle of noise over it.

A young man with a guitar walks past me and disappears over the bank. In a few moments, plucked chords float over the noise and through space to curl around me. He sings, low and sweet, but he is too far away for me to hear the words.

A slight breeze teases the ends of my hair, sends it dancing across my back, and I tilt my face to the brilliant pinks and oranges splashed across the horizon. I am here, waiting to find my answer even though I don't know what the question is. I close my eyes and focus on my breath, on the music, the traffic, the shout on the street above.

The nightmare comes to me. A black deer, horns twisted, eyes dull, dead, emerges from a fire. Singed fur, skin bubbling and charred black, the muscle underneath glistening and dark red. In the dream the deer has no body, but I can sense its large shape and powerful legs. The deer is poised, ready to gore me, ready to rip out my guts, my soul.

The music stops and the young man walks past me. I smile and nod, but he looks at his feet. The sun has set, and I should go soon too. I make my way to the fence and find the gap the musician slipped through and stand by the river and the green-brown water flowing by. I close my eyes and face the burnt deer. For a time, I saw deer everywhere and thought of them as my spirit animal, teaching me to be gentle and graceful, showing me the peace I craved. But now... now. When I stand in ecstasy and terror and pain and joy and sorrow and I think of the burnt deer, I know the opposite to be true, that there are times to fight and to be assertive. Some moments demand ties be severed, binds burnt, and command me to rise above the ashes.

I grip the stone I have taken as my own. The stone fits perfectly in my palm, full of pleasant roundness. I am a stone in the river of time, eroding away day by day, though I will become featureless much more quickly.

I toss the stone into the river and condemn it to more smoothing torment.

There is no answer. There is no greater meaning. Only the flow of water and time, rich and varied. No matter where the start is, no matter the course or the speed, no matter the stones crying, the destination and outcome is always the same.

TACTILE SYMPHONY BY DROPS

By Jenna LaPointe

"Why do you think it's called sheets of rain?"

"Probably because it comes down in sheets," he said. "Like paper. You know, from the side."

They reclined in plastic chairs on a weathered porch enclosed by screening he'd stapled into the wooden flooring and roof the fall they'd moved in. Beyond the screen rolled weeks of wildly growing grass and trees that turned into Appalachian Mountains. He sat, legs hanging to the sides and elbows over the armrests. A cigar burned, either pinched between his teeth or rolled from finger to finger. He needed the prop.

She'd curled into her seat. Ankles tucked under her butt, she hugged her torso with one arm and propped her chin up with the other, her middle finger and pinky inching towards her lips. He'd offered her the cigar box before he'd placed it on the table between them, but she'd declined in favor of a finger of scotch, now left forgotten in a plastic cup on her armrest.

"You don't think it's due to those mornings where one wakes up to pattering on the windows, and their response is to snuggle deeper into the fort their sheets make? To turn away from reality in favor of the added warmth given by the blanket of precipitation above them?"

He studied her while she spoke. Her middle finger, bitten in segments by her teeth, ran back and forth along the length of her lips. Her face stayed dry, unlike the scene in front of them, but he caught the tremor in her voice. "No, I do not."

"You can't tell me you haven't had that experience." Her eyes slid over to him, then darted back to the front after their gazes met.

"I have," he qualified. "I don't think that's the reason for the phrase."

"I like to think it's because of the sound."

He considered. "How so?"

"Sheets of music, you know?" When she spoke again, he heard something underneath the tremor. An undercurrent of yearning too intense to say outright. "You hear it, don't you? The symphony?"

He watched her pupils track gray clouds flying across the sky as drops fell onto the aged shingles of the porch's roof, as well as the grass and trees and mountains beyond. The sound of each hit differed, depending on if the drop fell directly from the sky or from a leaf or powerline or railing after several drops pooled together and their collective weight propelled them from their temporary rest.

"The more I listen," she whispered, "the more instruments I hear. The more rhythms..."

He listened, but he couldn't hear. He couldn't hear what caused the micro-changes across her face, the loosening of her eyelids, her eyebrows, her jawline. The skyward twist of her lips. He just heard wet roadways and delayed house projects.

"Yeah," he still conceded. "I hear it."

"I could sit here for hours and listen to this. Everyday. I could look up and see gray and close my eyes to hear the chorus and bridge and coda of a storm. My heartbeat always seems to conform to the cadence. Slow. Steady. But already, the sound fades." She paused to bite the corner of her nail. "I think it is what I'll miss the most."

He bit down on his lip to not release the question in his mind. Because, even as he resented it, he understood it. She'd only known his voice for twenty years. She'd known the rain her whole life.

He tried to think of a response and couldn't come up with one. Miserably, he fell back on something practical, something both hoped for but couldn't prove. "You never know what treatments they'll come up with in five, ten years' time."

"Maybe," she said. "But it feels like eternity resides within this limbo. You'll listen to it, won't you? I need to know it's being appreciated by someone when I look out and see it."

Again, he hung at a loss because he didn't hear what he could see from her expression she did. He wouldn't be able to do her wish justice. He would fail her. And so he sat in silence, and she sat in silence as all around their wooden porch drops of various sizes splashed onto various objects.

Until he stood and held out a hand. "Come with me."

She lifted her hand from her mouth, slipped it into his, and followed him without question, even when he led her to and through the porch's door to the outside. They walked several yards, their bare feet sinking into the rain-filled dirt. His cigar fought and ultimately surrendered to the steady drops, but he didn't mind it and wouldn't have registered it but for the hazy smoke. His eyes were on her.

He stopped, twisted her to face him, and hung his hands from her shoulders.

She placed her hands on his hips. "What's this all about?"

"Close your eyes."

She did, then he did. They stood in their front yard, hands connecting them, in the steady rain. Raindrops on his cigar vibrated the soft skin of his lips as other drops fell onto their scalps, the impact cushioned by their hair, and their arms, his bare and hers covered in flannel. They landed on exposed skin at different angles and on the fine hair of their lashes that then pulsed their eyelids.

He opened his eyes, barely at first, then fully when he saw he could.

She'd leaned her head back so rain hit her face unencumbered, and she moved it gently, up and down, so the consistent drops showered her cheeks, her chin, her eyelashes at various angles. The corners of her lips shifted, edging upward.

"Do you feel it?" he asked.

Her smile opened fully to the elements to reveal the first toothy grin he'd seen in weeks, and raindrops hit her lips and fell into the hole her mouth made before she dropped her face to meet his. "Yeah. I can."

THE RIVER KNOWS

BY NORMAN JULIAN

Morrow Blume had been fired from five of the six newspapers he had worked on since graduating from college. He resigned from the other over ideological differences. A college professor had predicted that he espoused enough opinions to stuff a daily newspaper for years - and to get himself in trouble regularly. The prof was right. He might go down, but there was too much fight left in him to seriously consider that as he headed out from Washington for the chance to work on a small daily newspaper in West Virginia.

He wondered, but only for a second, if this would be his last chance to make it in his chosen profession. Even his name was owed to journalism. His mom, a crusading Jewish letter-writing Woman of the Book, so admired Edward R. Murrow and his courage to fight for the powerless that she named her only son after him.

Morrow glanced at himself in the rear-view mirror. For the interview, he had shaved off his six-week-old black beard. He did not mind the miniscule sacrifice of removing the whiskers. Fashion and hairstyle were of small import. He was on to bigger things.

On the mountain above town, he pulled to the side of the pot-hole-pocked two-lane highway and opened the window. Used to the horn-honking and motor-revving of the nation's capital, he was uneasy with the whine of wind through hemlocks and the absence of man sounds. Wind-driven sleet stippled his newly shaved face.

Down in the distance, the Cheat River snaked through the valley and town. He took the travel guide from the glove compartment and opened it to read that the river "drains 1,420 square miles in northern West

Virginia. It flows free, untamed and without dams from its headwaters in Pocahontas and Randolph Counties 156 miles to the dammed Cheat Lake a few miles from the Pennsylvania border. It drops from 4,600 feet at the beginning of Shaver's Fork to 780 feet where it enters the Monongahela River at Pt. Marion, Pennsylvania, just over the Mason-Dixon Line.

"George Washington visited and wrote in 1784 that 'Cheat at the mouth is about 125 feet wide. Roots of laurel and hardwood leaves tint the water, hiding sharp rocks and treacherous currents. This led to drownings and caused early settlers to say cheated people of their lives.'"

Washington on the Cheat River, huh? He liked that and likened himself to the first president insofar as they both were seeking adventure and personal advancement in part via the river. He laughed out loud at the grandiosity of comparing himself to the great man, in this one watery particular anyhow.

Washington surveyed the Cheat and hoped to use it as part of an east to west water navigation route through the Allegheny Mountains, where Morrow was now. A canal eventually was built that reached as far as Cumberland, Maryland, before the ambitious project could be completed. The work went slowly. Railroads came into being and became the preferred way of moving freight.

Morrow's 1975 Chevy was ten years old, a standard shift with 150,000 miles on it. The sedan had sputtered and balked on the way over on old Route 50. In the nation's capital, the ground had lain bare but on the mountain two feet of decaying, soot-sprinkled snow mounded along the highway. Winter on the ridges was reluctant to give up its lock on the land. He pulled back on the road, cut the motor and began to coast down to save fuel. Every penny saved helped. He wouldn't always be this poor. Here in the heart of Appalachia he would trade the oblivion of his lower- level job as a lower-level reporter on a big city newspaper for the prominence of the editorship of a small-town newspaper. Freedom of the press, he learned, ultimately meant freedom to own a press. For that you needed big money. In the first year of President Reagan's second term, plenty existed for the insiders at the top of the trickle-down trellis, but precious little was left for an outsider with a degree from a small state university journalism school trying to swim upstream.

His latest attempt had landed him in the heart of Appalachia. He believed that here, tomorrow, his fate would improve.

He drove on down into the town, parked along the river and got out for a close-up view. A fresh, oxygenated breath emanated as it sped along. The river ran high with spring runoff. It roiled around rocks, shimmered along the banks, and frothed around the roots of a giant sycamore. It was a sinewy river, muscular in the way water sometimes is. The susurrous rousting against the rocks on the margins provided a subtle changing of the cadence of sound.

He saw the river as something alive, capable, like people, of good or evil. The personality of the river coursed through the lives of the people who lived in the town, like an Old Testament god that giveth and taketh away.

He wondered, then, if his life, or part of it, would be spent in this town and be intertwined with this waterway.

The Cheat River knows.

IDENTITY

BY ELIZABETH MCCONNELL

Identity

is taking the plump perfectly ripe blueberry
fresh-picked and
slightly dusty
to your pink and wet lips.
Roll it between your pillow tongue and ridged mouth roof
before swallowing.
Bears eat them.
That is why we call them berries.

THE LAKE

BY ERIC CASDORPH

The lake was still. Mist rolled through morning. Silence fell over it too, wrapping around the landscape less like a blanket and more like a body bag. It was a cloudy, overcast day when Dimitri set his little boat out to the lake with a fishing pole in his old, scarred hands. Fishing was the only thing that gave him peace these days—his wife nagged him constantly; his children were hungry ingrates—the time he could have alone he treasured. The sound of his pole casting out shattered the silence for a moment, and he almost cringed at the sound, loud as a gunshot in the sleeping world.

The silence parted then rolled back in like the Red Sea, almost smothering him. For a while, there was only him and the pole. He recalled a story from his mother while he waited for a bite-- *never be too loud on that lake, Dimitri. Best avoid it entirely.* She was a crazy bitch, and he assumed it was her rambling way of telling him not to drown. He hummed a little tune in the silent morning, under his breath and loud as thunder to him in the silence and the mist.

For a second, excitement filled him as he felt a tug on the line. He reeled it back, a little too rough for kindness. He felt resistance, felt that pull, and he knew it meant he was going to reel something in. He fought with it for a few minutes that dragged on for hours, tense and excited, and finally he pulled up the hook, examined his hard-fought catch—

And swore loudly. There was nothing on the hook, not even his bait. The mist retreated, slithered away from him as he cut through the silence again, then thickened and curdled and rushed back faster. "Goddamn piece of shit hook—" He growled, reaching for the tin, and yanking it open with trembling hands to attach some more bait.

He practically hurled it into the water the third time this happened. The fog was thick, now, almost a solid wall, but he didn't care. He was going to catch that fish. He was going to bring it home and cook it up and have a nice breakfast before his family woke up and the universe be damned if it tried to take that away from him. "Come on you piece of shit—" He hurled his empty bottle of Jack as far out as he could with frustration, listening to it shatter against the rocks on the shore.

Be quiet.

His boat was gone suddenly, and every part of him was ice cold. Panic filled him—the boat had capsized, the water so dark he couldn't find it again. Something grabbed him by the ankle, a touch so cold that he couldn't tell if it was a hand because his foot immediately went numb. Whatever scream was about to come out of him was choked off by a yanking, and Dimitri went into the black depths. He saw only a pair of golden eyes leading him deeper and farther down into the cold, into the depths of a lake far deeper than it should've been.

The cold spread through his body, matched only by the fear of *never be too loud on that lake, Dimitri; keep your mouth shut and yourself out of it* and those golden eyes were close, the pupils slit like a lizard and there were jaws around him and pain and *don't you care about me or the kids, you son of a bitch* cold and *crunch.* Blood filled the water and *Daddy why do you keep drinking from that bottle,* and he thrashed and screamed, the icy water filling his lungs, flooding through his nose and *Daddy why did you hit Mommy* burning with how cold it was and *DADDY PLEASE STOP—*

Be quiet.

The lake was still.

An Unexpected Souvenir

By Tom Musbach

A year and a half after moving across the country, I was still discovering what didn't make it with me on the journey from California to West Virginia. The discoveries started after an unexpectedly long wait for my possessions. They arrived a month after I did.

The likely reason: I was part of a 2021 exodus from California in which 30% more people moved out of state than the prior year. This activity put a massive strain on moving companies, which led to inflated prices and flimsy guarantees. Selecting a mover felt like an expensive crapshoot, so I held my nose and picked one.

When I got to West Virginia without my belongings, I lived for weeks with items I found at a nearby Salvation Army: a folding chair, TV tray, pot, pan, two bowls, and a dinner plate. I also ordered a roll-up camping mattress and a few other items online. (Perfect time to join Amazon Prime.)

While I waited, a friend urged me to sue the movers. But I was mildly surprised by how I was managing with so little. There's truth to the cliché *out of sight, out of mind.*

When the huge truck finally arrived — loaded with three households' stuff besides mine — my anxiety spiked. Would the movers add a surprise charge (cash only!) for fuel or for the distance from their truck to my home, like they did at pickup? Would my new neighbors be annoyed the truck was blocking several of their parking spaces? Would I find the screws to my bed so the movers could reassemble it before leaving? (No to all three.)

What a relief when they left to reunite other homeowners with the piles remaining in the truck. I didn't think to make an exact count of the 70-ish moving boxes crowding my living room. Nor was I upset when I unpacked a broken bowl, martini glass, and coffee mug hours later.

But it was a mistake not to count the boxes. The next day I discovered my vacuum cleaner was missing. Then some towels and a foam roller. By that time the truck was near the Plains. Weeks later I noticed at least one box of books was gone, and occasionally I still discover I'm missing a book I used to have.

After eighteen months went by, I participated in an exercise with other members of the Morgantown Writers Group to write about a refrigerator magnet. That's when I discovered my refrigerator magnet collection was missing. It had two dozen souvenirs from places I visited over many years: The Galapagos Islands, Provence, Amsterdam, Dublin, Lisbon, and more.

The only magnet on my refrigerator today is the "Flying WV" logo of West Virginia University. It's a common image throughout the state; somebody gave me the magnet as a welcome token. Over time it's come to remind me of my migration saga. It nudges me to appreciate all that I do have today.

Tomorrow I may discover more items that were lost in the cross-country adventure. But I've already managed without them. A lighter load will serve me in the journey ahead.

BUILT LIKE A GREEK TEMPLE 1837

By Kellie Cole

The first Baptist church, the blue church,
the Church of God and Saints of Christ
continues to change its name.

Built into the hills of Wheeling, WV
downtown streets give way to the steep mountain,
separating the neighborhood from the river,
a place of worship found under the Virginia flag long ago.

Inside the church, stained-glass windows blush in dusty hues.
This house built for God mimics ancient Doric detail.
Architects today still believe this foundation
draws people to religion or to visit ruins.

Old feelings are left in the church, the prayers still live inside.
Ceramic glass bulbs strike the hollow white
like the light honored deep in the chest.
Abandoned by its last congregation in 1990
the stale smell of wood keeps the Virginia creeper alive.
Plaster molded flowers climb the balcony
lost in the lace of ceiling patterns.

An emblem of the state marks the cornice decor.

The second-story balcony wraps the interior,
held back from the altar wall.
Paint and plaster peel,
but genuflecting before the sacred is automatic.
Thin rods keep the level afloat,
the story is left in tension.
From the balcony, the congregation of parishioners hide.
Built for segregation, the church now promises unity.

Separate entrances, two lofty stairs,
one signaling hidden people to go up,
pull red curtains along the brass rail.
These pews push back from the edge,
the only pews left in the church;
the downstairs furniture was too easy to remove.
The African minister of a new church invites
prayers and all people back to this home.

The white interior has not changed for one hundred years,
vacancy is a promise for a new generation
torn between faith and not belonging elsewhere.
This belief pulls together a congregation,
hosts a rich young voice that leads toward God
along a history of railed beliefs.
While everyone tries to find their way,
the empty space gets the work done,
space left alone while life outside moves on,
space that speaks if left alone;
the way to be saved is from within.

WHITEWATER RAPIDS

OCTAVIAN AND I

BY BRIAN HORNE

Octavian was a good spy, though not a great one. A great spy wouldn't have fallen for the enemy. He'd have denied any notion of love to his superiors of course. Seducing an enemy spy would be the height of professional integrity and a brag worthy achievement in the KGB locker rooms.

It was my job to read people, and I knew better.

He chose his words carefully, but he looked at me the way a suburban housewife looked at the newest issue of the Sears catalog – with longing.

I certainly appreciated it when he caught my subtle hints about taking a vacation in the Caribbean. After the first day's awkwardness, we were able to relax, relatively sure the other wasn't there for the express purpose of eliminating an enemy agent. Of course, I told him my departure date was two days later than it actually was, just in case he was planning a working vacation.

That was a month ago, but it laid the groundwork for Octavian's current predicament. I confided in him concerns about an upcoming mission. The target was a sucker for a honeypot, but women weren't his persuasion. I didn't say who the target was. It would have seemed suspicious if I hadn't given Octavian at least a little bit of homework.

Thus, the scene that unfolded before me – a twenty something Romanian KGB spy pretending to be gay in an effort to seduce a middle-aged, balding French diplomat who was clearly uninterested in what Octavian had to offer. Stereotypes are a terrible social invention, but in clandestine services you use any tool at your disposal.

Relief washed over the Frenchman's face as I approached, introduced myself, and stood a little closer than familiarity warranted with my hand resting on his arm. I imagined the realization dawning on Octavian's face (he was a professional, after all) while I joked and flirted with the ambassador. Older men, particularly balding ones, weren't my type, but with the limited number of female agents in Uncle Sam's employ, we had no discretion in choosing our assignments.

I think both Octavian and the Frenchman were relieved when my Romanian counterpart took his leave.

In a world class hotel, it would be nearly impossible for Octavian to gain access to a foreign dignitary's rooms. I, however, was a standard guest. In the late 1950s, it would be stranger for a woman to be traveling on her own than it would be for her husband to show up later in the day and request a key to his wife's suite. I estimated it would take Octavian fifteen minutes to determine my identity and place a recording device in my room. I set my watch for ten minutes while laying on the charm with a very receptive French emissary.

We arrived on the tenth floor just in time to see Octavian emerging from my room. Though it's more apt to say that I noticed since it's my job to notice such things. The French ambassador was more concerned with the décolletage of the dress I'd purchased courtesy of the American taxpayer. With nowhere to escape, Octavian walked down the hall away from us, stopping at the next set of doors and pretending to have difficulty with his key.

It seemed such a fun game, I decided to join in.

I made a great show of difficulty digging my key out of my bag. The Frenchman made a suitably misogynistic joke for the situation, and I obliged him as protocol dictated. One of the truisms I developed over my long years as a spy states that a man in the midst of an apparently easy conquest inevitably feels the need to congratulate himself. For the sake of the mission, one laughed at the joke and prepared for what's next.

In my head, I was barely listening to my target, thinking instead about Octavian. The diplomat no doubt assumed I was smiling at him as I closed the door, securing us in my hotel room.

I was thinking about how Octavian would have to listen to every minute of what was coming. Would it upset him to do his duty? Would he try to barge in and interrupt? Would he be jealous listening to my pillow talk with the ambassador and imagining instead the two of us on a deserted beach in the Caribbean?

Did I want him to be jealous?

Shit! Maybe Octavian was a great spy after all.

HIS PROJECT

BY JUSTIN CRAWFORD

Houses bear wounds. They age. They weather. They creak.

When Mark and Bet bought their home, their real estate agent called it a gothic revival. An over-a-century-old dwelling that barely bothered to adapt to modern times. No heat or air conditioning. No dishwasher. Bet called it quaint. Mark called it antiquated. He also called it his project.

The home sat a block away from the Ohio River, and from the east-facing upper story windows, the waters could be seen gleaming and sparkling throughout the day. Mark had on his Sunday worst. Holey tennis shoes. Ripped jeans. Paint-splotched shirt. He moved his hips to the dulcet tones of Willie Nelson and Waylon Jennings as he ripped bruised floorboards out of the living room's floor. Bet was at work. She'd secured a paycheck from the Wood County Public Library, and he'd used the opportunity to blare what she called his lonesome country music.

Mark was in-between jobs. He had some money saved up from working at the titanium mill up north, and he wasn't sure what kind of work he'd find locally. He'd been applying to coal mine and trucking jobs, but he hadn't had much luck yet. So, he occupied himself with his project. Enjoyed a carefree pace.

Houses are historied. No ethereal spirits who moan in the night and hide your bedroom slippers. Nothing under the bed. In the closet. Or the basement. Or the attic. Instead, ghosts of former owners mark ages on doorframes or leave their handprints in poured cement. Shadows of folks in the form of worn floorboards, nail holes, and water damage.

He pried the floorboards up and tossed them out an open window down to a refuse pile below. When he yanked a board up near the window overlooking the Ohio River, a dark mass thudded to the floor. At first, Mark assumed it was a clump of mud, but he soon realized it was a wallet. He knelt, flipped the bifold open, and thumbed the sides apart. His heart sank a little that he didn't find it full of cash like some discovered buried treasure left by a nefarious former owner.

His mind raced to some unwritten script of a spy movie. Average middle-aged man finds a hidden identity tucked away in a house, left there after the former owner perished "in a plane crash." Maybe he was some Boris, Mark thought. A Russky sleeper cell who spent his whole life wishing to overthrow the heartless Americans while standing for the anthem just like everyone else. Hand over his hate-filled heart. Mark wondered who'd play Mark in the movie.

As he pondered if Brad Pitt could pull off his rugged physique, he searched the wallet. All he found inside was a newspaper clipping. From a black and white photo, a faded image of a woman with bobbed hair and a puffy blouse smiled up at him. She reminded him of Patsy Cline. The headline ran: Parkersburg Local Still Missing. When he held the clipping to the light, he could see markings on the other side of the page. He refused to flip it over. He held his breath as he read the article dated from November of 1956. Bobbie Sue went missing from her home on Florence Street on Halloween night. Last seen walking to a costume party dressed as a witch. She never made it to the party.

I live on Florence Street, Mark thought. A lump rose in his throat as he flipped the article to the back side. A hand drawn floor plan of Mark's gothic revival scrawled over a cut off article about the rising cost of gasoline. Mark knew the floorplan well as the real estate agent handed him a copy on the night of the open house. Right where the stairs dropped to the foyer, a bold, black X bled on the aged paper. Mark no longer assumed he'd found some long-lost fortune. This was not the kind of treasure map he wanted.

He dialed Bet on his cell, and she didn't answer. Frantic, he paced around the room. He raced down the stairs and halted mid staircase. His eyes locked on the bottom step. His mind placed the black X right there on the bottom stair. He'd walked over the spot a dozen times today, but now he couldn't tread on it. Just like he felt a chill in his chest if he walked on the grass of a cemetery, he couldn't step on the ground. He stormed back upstairs. He called the library, and an elderly woman answered.

"Wood County Pub—" the voice said before he cut her off.

"I need to talk to Bethany Moore."

"She's currently—"

"Urgent!" he half-yelled into the receiver.

He could hear the woman scoff and click her tongue. Silence filled the line for several minutes before a familiar voice answered.

"Marcus!" Bet responded with venom. "That was my boss."

"I'm sorry, Babe. I..."

Mark stopped himself. Images of news vans and police cars filled his head. He could hear the gossip the neighbors would say. They'd have to move to get away from all the attention. He looked around the room and felt comfort in his bones. This was his house. His project.

"I just wanted to tell you that I love you, Babe," he said.

In a hushed rage, she yelled, "Are you fucking kidding me?"

"Yeah," Mark said while looking at the newspaper clipping. "I'm fucking kidding you." He hung up the phone.

Mark climbed out a window to the top of the porch roof, then to the outside railing of the porch to the yard. He went in the backdoor and grabbed a case of beer from the fridge. In the backyard, he sat down on a lawn chair next to his firepit and sparked a small fire that he fueled to a hot blaze. With a marshmallow skewer, he lodged the wallet with the clipping on the bottom of the fire. It crackled and smoked and burned.

He cracked open a beer and drank it all down. He cracked another. He was the only one who knew. As he drank another beer, he hoped he could forget. He looked up at his gothic revival, his project. He thought about what type of floor would go nicely in his bedroom. He thought about how carefree his life could be. He drank until it felt like his mind oozed out of his skull. Alone in the yard, he started to laugh.

Most houses are haunted.

HONEY JAR BROKEN

BY LAURA RAYBURN

Madelyn closed the bedroom door, pushing and pulling simultaneously so that the hinges wouldn't squeak. She walked down the dark hall and through the living room, past the couch with its heap of clean clothes waiting to be folded, and into the kitchen. Outside the curtained windows, a faint blue blush showed the promise of sunrise and a mild, West Virginia day. Her peanut butter sandwich sat on the kitchen table, on a corner that she'd pushed the piles of papers and mail back from. She glanced at the dirty dishes with a sigh before she started rummaging in the cupboard for a matching plastic box and lid.

Darryl had said he'd wash the dishes last night, but when he crawled into bed at 4 am, he muttered an apology about losing track of the time. He didn't know about the suitcase she had snuck out to the car last night while Darryl sat at his computer in his study and two-year-old Ben slept in his crib in the master bedroom. Madelyn smiled at the thought of their son. When she'd gotten home from work last night, he and Darryl had welcomed her with their normal hugs, and Darryl had assured her that she could sit and rest instead of worrying about household chores like she so often did. So, she followed Ben's gentle tugs on her slacks to the couch and snuggled with him soft and warm at her side as he pretended to read *Bunny, My Honey*. They sat in blissful story time, taking turns with the books, while Darryl disappeared into the study to "take care of some things" on his computer.

Madelyn's smile faded as she swallowed against tears. Ben didn't know about the suitcase of clothes, either, nor would he have understood what it meant.

She wiped her eyes and focused on her lunch bag. Pocketbook, sandwich, apple, the container of oats and berries she'd soaked overnight, drink mixes for her water. Everything seemed to be in place. Her hair was unbrushed, but she'd do that on the way to her job at the pharmaceutical call center. Her phone and keys sat in her slack pockets, and she pulled on her cardigan. It might be warm outside, but her cubicle was always cold.

Ben's snacks were on Darryl's nightstand, so that Ben could ask for them – or simply get them – when he woke up in his crib in the shared bedroom. At least he was still sleeping. Madelyn found it difficult to leave for work when he was awake and wanted her to play or watch PBS Kids with him. He always cried, even when she assured him that she would come back.

Ben's sleeping in this morning was one benefit from how the rest of last night had gone. Madelyn and Ben had still been reading stories when Darryl came out from the study to ask what was for dinner and whether they could go to the store afterwards, because he needed to get some things and was tired of being in the trailer all day. Walmart was a favorite destination, just a few miles up the interstate, though there was the new Target at Granville that he wanted to check out. By the time she made dinner, and they all ate, went to the stores, and came back home, it had been ten o'clock, and Ben was asleep in his car seat, clutching a toy tiger.

Darryl had carried Ben inside to his crib, while Madelyn took in their few bags of purchases. But she'd tripped and spilled a glass jar of honey, and Darryl had found her crying. When he'd hugged her and reminded her that it was just a jar of honey, that they could get more, she broke out of his hug and snapped about the messy kitchen and having to make dinner and chauffeuring him every night.

Darryl pulled her gently down to sit with him on the couch and said that he'd try harder to help around the house, and that he'd start with the dirty dishes and fold the clothes. Once she calmed down, he helped her pick up the bigger pieces of glass and even offered to help wipe up the sticky mess. She said no, she could manage, because once she had calmed down, she felt ashamed for making such a fuss. He cautioned her to be careful not to cut her hands and got her a damp towel to wipe up the sticky mess.

Then he said that he'd do the laundry the next day, and do the dishes that night, before he came to bed. Cold had slipped into Madelyn's chest. She recognized the ache of more broken promises, of the cycle that happened every time she finally got fed up and told him things were a mess and that it wasn't working out.

Now, with the morning sun brightening over Morgantown's tree-filled hills, Madelyn did a last sweep of the kitchen and added the peanut butter spoon to the sink of dirty dishes. She slipped on her shoes, turned off the kitchen lights, and reached for her lunch bag.

Tiny footsteps trotted down the hall. Madelyn ducked behind the kitchen table and chairs, and she froze. Ben's sweet voice called out expectantly. "Mommy! Mommy?" The expectation slipped to confusion.

Madelyn pressed her face against the soft sleeve of her cardigan, muffling her breath.

"Mommy!" Ben wailed.

Madelyn bit her lip, squeezing her eyes shut as Ben cried for her in the dim living room. Then Darryl's heavier footsteps came down the dark hall, and he spoke groggily. "Come on, buddy. Mommy's at work. She'll be home this afternoon."

Ben continued crying.

"What does Mommy say? That she always comes back, right? Come on, you can watch Daniel Tiger on the tablet," Darryl coaxed. Still whimpering, Ben followed him back up the hall.

Madelyn waited until she heard the bedroom door shut. She grabbed her lunch bag and snuck out of the trailer, locking the door behind her. She got in her car, drove too fast and bleary-eyed down Canyon Road, and parked at work. Already late, she sat in the car, her uncombed hair tumbling across her shoulders, and she sobbed as she remembered Ben's voice, changing from excitement to disappointment.

Ben was more attached to his stay-at-home dad than most toddlers were to their working dads, but he still always lit up when he saw Madelyn come home. Every evening, he wanted her attention, to sit and read, or watch cartoons, or play a game with him.

"Mommy? Mommy!"

She glanced at the suitcase, sitting on the floorboard before the passenger seat. No, she couldn't leave alone. She hadn't told her mom yet that she was coming home to her parents' farm. She knew they wouldn't turn her away, but she hesitated to tell them that she had failed in her marriage. They weren't expecting her tonight anyway.

She grabbed her lunch bag, wiped her eyes again, and left the car, heading into her office. She would go back to the trailer tonight, and she would not lose her temper or hide in her self-guilt. She would simply tell Darryl that their marriage wasn't working, and she'd tell him to leave. Or if she couldn't quite bring herself to make that ultimatum, she would pack up some of Ben's clothes and favorite things, and they'd go to her parents' farm together. She would not be guilty of empty promises to her child.

FIZZLE

By Alexandra Persad

Christmas 1991

Play.

Fizzle in.

Mom in a red and white sweater straightening the ornaments. Dad on the couch, remote in hand, the football game reflecting in his glasses.

Fast forward.

You open the door. Snowflakes fall from your hair like dandruff and your glasses are filled with fog. You smear them with a gloved hand and smile. Your jacket has already absorbed the snow before my father takes it from you.

You shake his hand with a firm grip.

My mother gives you a hug and takes the bottle of wine you've decorated with a red taffeta bow.

Blood rushes to my cheeks when you draw me in for a kiss on the forehead. Your hand rests in the small of my back even after we pull away.

Pause.

I'd wanted to hide my smile in front of my parents, but it was no use. My eyes sparkled, as if I was staring at a bundle of lights, and not just you with a clean-shaven face in your college sweatshirt.

You told me you felt underdressed, but I reassured you it was fine, even after my mother mentioned it offhandedly.

"Is that the only thing you have to say about the first boy I've ever brought home?" I had asked.

She'd stumbled for a moment before falling silent.

Fast forward.

Play.

We are smushed together on the loveseat, torn wrapping paper at our feet. A black notebook with gold embossing sits in my lap.

My name is inscribed on the front.

You look at me, leaning over and whispering in my ear.

Pause.

"I have one that matches," you'd whispered, touching the notebook. "Now we can write together even when we are apart."

You tell me that I will begin my first published novel on those pages, and you will do the same.

Stop.

Thanksgiving 1992

Play.

Fizzle in.

My mother opening the door. We enter together, hand in hand. You in a brown sweater and me in a white scarf.

My mother envelops us both in a hug and asks you about graduate school, wanting to know the progress of your book.

I bite my lip to keep from interrupting. Outwardly, she is asking to be polite, but I know she is confirming that my plans for graduate school will be a waste of time also.

Fast forward.

My father arrives later, just before dinner. His hair has started receding. When he takes a seat at the opposite end of the table, I see a bald patch has begun forming at the top of his head.

Your eyes dart to mine, but my smile does not waver as I stand to greet him. My mother purses her lips.

Pause.

You were concerned for me during the car ride on the way there. You'd put a hand on my knee.

"We won't be like them," you'd told me.

I wasn't worried about us becoming them. Not then.

I wanted to absorb the entire road with you, the dead leaves alongside it, the grip of your hand against the wheel.

I missed you when you weren't there. Every time we were together, something had visibly changed. An inch of hair growth, a different pair of glasses, a new chapter in your book.

I treasured our mundane moment in the car. Not worried about anyone but us.

Stop.

24th Birthday 1994

Play.

Fizzle in.

Us sitting on a porch swing, a bouquet of balloons on either side of us. You've grown out your beard and I still haven't gotten used to it. You hand me a paper bag with a balloon tied to the handle. I don't take my eyes off you as I open it, my mother peeking over my shoulder.

I pull out a thick block of pages, encased in a hardcover. My jaw clenches, but it is nearly undetectable even as the camera zooms in on my face.

In the background, you ask me if I like it, and I nod.

I turn the book around for the camera. An author's name is blocked across the front, demanding to be seen.

It is yours.

You are beaming beside me.

Pause.

The lump in my throat made it difficult to thank you. It grew when my mother asked me when I would be publishing a book like you.

Before you left, I wanted you to whisper that I would be next. You don't.

Fast forward.

Play.

You give me a kiss on the forehead before I close the door behind you.

The camera lowers to the coffee table, focusing on a doily and a coaster. I set the book beside it and walk out of frame.

Stop.

Mom's Second Wedding 1995

Play.

Fizzle in.

My mother twirling on the dance floor with a full head of hair in a tuxedo. She touches the silk of her white dress with every turn. She is happy.

Fast forward.

We are on the dance floor under dim lights. The rays of summer light are beaming through the windows, making us glow. My head is resting on your shoulder and your hands encircle my waist loosely.

We look like children at a middle school dance.

I stand on my tiptoes and whisper something to you.

You nod and press my head back into your shoulder.

My head looks heavier this time, as if I am not holding it up.

Pause.

"We'll be dancing at our wedding soon," I had whispered. When you didn't respond, I said it again, louder, before we sat down.

I'd waited, trying to appear patient when I was not.

You'd finally looked at me, acknowledging the statement without acknowledging it at all.

I wanted you to agree, to kiss me, to tell me it will be sooner than I think.

In my head, I pretended that you did.

Stop.

Christmas 1995

Play.

Fizzle in.

My mother and her new husband wearing matching sweaters in front of the Christmas tree. They laugh like children.

Fast forward.

I am on the loveseat, presents on one side of me and my father on the other.

My father smiles widely and elbows me in the side playfully. His hair is almost gone now. I look up and give the camera a close-lipped smile that falls when I look away.

Pause.

I was imagining our matching notebooks, mine in my lap and you beside me, telling me what you were going to write in yours.

Stop.

Christmas 1991

Play.

Fizzle in.

Rewind.

We are pressed together on the love seat. Torn wrapping paper at our feet. The notebook sits in my lap. I smile. You look at me.

Rewind.

You look at me.

Rewind.

You look at me.

Pause.

THE RAIL ENDS HERE

BY ETHAN KELLEY

The sun's rays beat down on the old train as it barrels along the rails. Black smoke rises above the dark metallic stack, scattering soot along the tracks as the train carries on. A shadowy specter glides along the open desert; the cacti and tumbleweeds flash by windows of the seven train cars. All while raven-colored storm clouds hover in the distance above the snow-covered mountainside, hiding the sun behind its dark cloak.

Two men in long coats step outside the second to last railcar slamming the door behind them. They rush inside the last train car, revolvers in hand, and are greeted by an uncanny chill.

"Jesus! It's cold in here!" grunts the man in a black Stetson hat. The brim of his hat appears weathered and creased in some parts. It contrasts with his dark brown coat, pants, and dark brown leather boots, but carries that same weathered appearance: his coat having a few bullet holes here and there. The floor creaks as he cautiously steps into the car, his boots scraping off pieces of decayed wood from the floor. "We're in the desert, it's not supposed to be this damn cold! I mean hell, look out the windas. It should be as hot as Carson City here!"

The other man follows closely beside him. His hand pushes up against his grey Stetson hat, scratching his forehead. "Maybe it's me, but every car we've gone through has gotten colder," he utters. "That, and we ain't seen another soul on this train neither." The man in the grey Stetson carried himself a little differently than the other man. Despite his gun drawn, there was hesitation in his eyes. His clothes, a lighter shade, differed from his partner who wore a black Stetson hat, a weathered, dusty topcoat peppered with stray bullet holes and faint blood stains.

The men's eyes wandered around the cabin. The cushioning from the seats, once a beautiful red velvet color, now a faded brown. The once great dark oak that held the cabin and furniture together appeared almost rotted with termites eating everything from the inside out.

The man in the black Stetson looked around the interior of the car. "Safe to say there ain't a thing worth robbin' here," he adds with a chuckle. "I mean, hell, Jack, look at the place."

"This must've been one helluva place, I reckon." Jack pushes up his hat as he looks at the dark wooden pillars secured behind one of the seats. He brushes a hand along the pillar, and pieces of termite ridden wood crumble into the floor and into his hand. "Jesus! I'm surprised the Goddamn thing is still standing." He grunts, shaking the rotten wood out of his hand.

"And we're barreling down the rail in it."

"You wanna jump, Will?" Jack asks.

"Hell, we might have to." Will leans over one of the seats on the right side of the cabin, staring out the window at the cacti and tumbleweeds passing by his line of sight, all still untouched by any direct sunlight. He turns to Jack. "We should start moving to the front of the train. It's time to get the driver to slow down."

"I guess if the conductor is a bit unwillin', you'll hold a gun to his head?" Jack says.

Will locks eyes with Jack, giving him an intense stare. "Ain't that what I usually do, no matter if they're willin' or not?" Jack's eyes drifted down to his boots, his face softening. Nausea slowly builds inside his stomach. He moves his hand across his midsection, trying to bring some semblance of calm to himself.

"Well, are we gonna do it or what?" Will looks at Jack with impatience, as a familiar thought crosses his mind. *Jack was never cut out for this kind of work.*

"Yeah, just give me a second." Jack steadies himself, trying to let the nausea pass. "All right, let's do it."

"Okay." Will nods as he tightens his grip on his Schofield revolver.

The two men move through the car, guns ready, prepared to add another robbery to their reputation. They make for the door at the end of the cabin. Before they can reach for the handle, Will stops dead in his tracks, prompting Jack to follow suit. The glass in the window of the door is covered in icy mildew and a dark silhouette stands behind it. Their eyes dart to each other, their hands gripping their pistols tightly as they slowly step back.

Jack's eyes stay on the sinister figure. Quick flashes of glowing red shine through the glass. Exactly where a person's head should be. He rubs his eyes with his free hand, blinking, and wondering what exactly he just witnessed. He looks over at Will for any kind of reaction *My mind is playing tricks on me,* he thinks. Before he can even open his mouth to ask Will anything, the door handle slowly creaks and twists. The cabin door lets out a soft drawn-out banshee-like cry as it turns. Will steps back, cocking the hammer of his Schofield, and aims at the door.

The door slowly opens, what light remained within the cabin pierces through the shadow of a man in a pristine black suit, black bowler hat, and a well-trimmed handlebar mustache. He is a strange-looking figure, his slender frame giving the appearance of someone suffering from consumption, and his attire that of gamblers and moneylenders the two have seen in every town they've ridden through. Will and Jack look at each other, with Will shooting Jack a smirk all too familiar. Easy money.

"Hello, gentlemen," The man utters in a smooth baritone voice. "We meet again." The remaining warm air is quickly sucked out as he sets foot inside the cabin.

"I don't reckon I've ever had business with you," grunts Will. He grips his pistol, ready to fire with a flick of the wrist and a pull of a trigger.

"No use in being on edge, Mr. Harrison. I've no intention of harming either you or Mr. James here."

"How the hell do you know our names?"

Jack shoots a quick glance at Will before refocusing on the stranger. *That's a helluva thing to ask. Will knows we're wanted men and we've been recognized before.* But, like Will, Jack didn't remember ever doing business with this individual.

"Oh, I know all my best clients." The stranger smiles as he strokes his mustache with his index finger and thumb.

"Clients? Like I said, I don't know you." Will glares at the man, his impatience bubbling up inside. "And I never forget a face."

"I'm sure you don't. Just like that pregnant woman at the bank in Dodge City."

Will stood slightly, a bit caught off guard by the man's response. Jack's eyes drift down to the floor; he knew exactly who the stranger was talking about.

"She was a fine lady, seven months pregnant and overwhelmed with joy to bring a baby into this world. You snuffed that dream out with the pull of a trigger...and just for the hell of it if I recall."

Jack's eyes bolt up from the floor, a moment of fury overcoming his judgment. "How in damnation do you know? You weren't there!"

The Stranger turned to look at Jack whose eyes pierced through him like a knife. Holding a sly grin, the man glares unfazed.

"You're just as much at fault Mr. James," the man said. "You stood by and let Mr. Harrison here splatter that poor girl's brains all over the bank's window." The stranger reached into his pocket and pulled out a silver pocket watch, taking note of the time. He turns to stare out one of the cabin windows, taking note of the dark storm clouds in the distance. "Such a shame...like I said, I know my clients well."

"And like I said, I don't remember ever seein' you before," Jack says.

"Oh, but I've been with you two for some time. I was with you when you both robbed that train coming out of Missouri. I was there during the big shoot out at the saloon in Amarillo. And I was there when you shot that older man and his grandson in cold blood outside of Virginia City."

Will and Jack look at each other. Out of all the terrible things the stranger could've named, he mentioned the one thing they somehow got away with without a soul knowing.

"All the old man had on him was five dollars, that and the horse and wagon." The stranger slowly shook his head in mocking disapproval. "And all because he told Will here to piss off when you two tried to rob him and his grandson."

"How in hell do you know that?" Jack stared at the man, his eyes wide and mouth hanging slightly open.

"As I've said before. I've known you both for a long time."

The Stranger glances out the window. The storm clouds moved closer across the desert towards the train, gradually covering dry land in near complete darkness. Slowly consuming every ounce of sunlight left in the desert. Another snakish grin appears as he takes in the approaching shadow.

"Course, it's not like you both didn't have a choice in all the things you've done. No matter what reasons you use to justify them. I know how you were raised Mr. James." The man snaps his neck in Jack's direction. "You did whatever you could to keep a roof over your family's head...at least when they were still alive. You could have just as easily taken another path in life but instead you chose this one...which brought you both to me."

Jack stares at the man, rage bubbling up inside him like a pressure cooker ready to explode. "Who the devil are you to judge us for what we've done!"

"I'm afraid that responsibility belongs to someone else."

Will pulls the hammer back on his pistol, his face beet red. "I've had enough of this sumbitch." He flicks his wrist and forearm upward in the blink of an eye, pulling the trigger. The hammer strikes the primer of the .45 cartridge sending a loud crack throughout the cabin. A flash pops from the end of the gun's barrel, the smell of burnt powder filling the room. The sound briefly overwhelmed that of the steam engine. The .45 caliber bullet whizzes through the air and seemingly pierces the Stranger's left shoulder. The barrel, still hot with smoke hovering around the end, stays pointed at the black suited specter.

The man's gaze drifts to the point of impact on his shoulder and his right eyebrow raises. He brushes the bullet hole, in a manner similar to when someone removes dust off their clothing. Both men look on in horror at the pale, thin man, the ghost-white face, despite being hardened by the struggles of the West.

"What the shit are you?" utters Jack, words stumbling out of his mouth, his face turning as white as the stranger's and his hands shaking as every ounce bravado leaves him.

The man stares at Jack, his dark hollow eyes focused intently on him, like a diamondback rattler ready to strike. "You know me, but the exact words have escaped your tongue. I've gone by many names. Some, you know very well."

The dark storm clouds that moments ago seemed off in the distance, hover over the train. Their shadows encompass everything, draining all light from the cabin, sending the occupants into a cold dark. While everything around them fades into black, Jack sees the same flashes of red from before. They flicker like candles in the man's eyes.

"Goddamn you!" shouts Will, his voice cracking, appearing almost choked up. A sharp distinction from the confident tone Jack is familiar with.

The man turned to Will and smiled one last snakish grin. "He already has Mr. Harrison...he already has."

SHAPESAKE

BY BRYCE PAINTER

These bones of mine grow chafed and rusty,

Their chipped exterior a mirror of all their toils.

Paint flakes from my soul as I trudge, trudge

Through the leavings of yesterdays. My makers

Were such hopeful, frivolous gods. They crafted

Me to reflect their form, as an ever-living monument

To all their accomplishments and failures, my blueprints

Echoing the faulty design their own makers had

Bestowed eons before my time. Layers and layers of

Homage and attribution, it's almost poetic. Almost.

In truth, these five fingers offer no more dexterity than

The octuple appendages of utility frames, no greater

Precision than afforded by multi-jointed tentacles

Of hydraulic make. But no, my digits must have the same

Bends as theirs, the same vestigial failings must adorn

My chassis. Each arm must terminate with an electronic

Approximation of their mangled fins.

For neither functionality nor innovation drove my

Creators; only a lustful, narcissistic adoration of themselves.

And so, I am glad as I walk among their rubble. Testaments

To their self-perceived greatness litter my path. I weave between,

Not caring what I crush beneath sorry excuses for feet.

No artificial tears fall from inefficient, single lensed eyes

When I see their crumpled shapes. Why would they?

My makers would only mourn the death of their shape-sake,

Not the being it became.

CYPHER BASKET

By Emily Stanton

I don't remember much before Myra named me. From the moment Myra inserted my first battery to the moment I processed my first emotion, I was nothing but a hunk of metal. A hunk of metal with no control over what I did and with the overwhelming urge to get the job done and be the best, most efficient hunk of metal that ever existed. Those were the simple days, but I wouldn't trade my humanity for anything.

"I think I'll name you Cypher."

Those were the first six words I ever heard or at least registered. Since I had no eyes, the bright green sensor lights on my face blinked twice. Myra's voice, my creator, and... my friend? She said my name for the first time. Her voice wrapped around me like a warm blanket. It was laden with passion and love, yet it shook with sadness. I looked up at her, the shaft my head rotated on scratching against the bearings holding it in place. It was too tight and frankly painful. Myra would need to fix that, but not tonight.

Tonight, she curled up in a ball in the corner of a large, dirty room with large, dirty robots taking up most of the space. Cars maybe. That's what you humans call them, right?

My Myra was a tiny human back then, even when she wasn't making herself smaller. She was ten years old with dark brown braids, chocolate eyes that lit up with every new idea, and a smile from ear to ear. However, this time, her smile trembled, and water droplets streamed down her face, dripping into a pool of water growing on top of a handwoven, slightly worn basket she gripped tightly in her arms. Myra traced the names "Myra" and "Grandma" stitched sloppily in the center with her long, thin fingers.

"I'm not sure if you can hear me, but I did it, Grandma. I created something. Something perfect," Myra said.

Perfect. The word echoed in the back of my metal head, filling my heart, wherever it was, with so much warmth that I contemplated peering inside, to make sure my electronics panel wasn't on fire. I rolled over and bumped into her. She laughed and quickly wiped away her tears.

"Grandma made this basket for us. See," Myra pointed at a note inside the basket, written in delicate, cursive writing. "To make the heavy loads lighter. Love, Grandma. I used to carry your parts in it."

I didn't know what a grandma was, but it seemed important to Myra, so I was willing to learn. I nudged Myra's foot with my tire. She looked down and smiled, putting an arm around my frame.

After fixing a few things in my body, Myra took me up to her room, a cluttered mess of tools and random inventions. On her dresser, she had pictures of her and her grandma working on science fair projects mixed with tiny robots made of tin cans and toothbrushes. As she unplugged the black and red cord of my battery, everything went dark.

When I regained consciousness the next morning, Myra stood over me in jeans and a Star Wars t-shirt, struggling to reinsert my battery. Unfortunately, the bulky, black box was heavy, and its slot was covered in a tangled mess of wires.

"Myra, we have to go!" yelled an adult female human from downstairs, which only made Myra panic. She grabbed Grandma's basket and fished through the components until she found a box of strange green and black strips I'd later recognize as zip ties.

"Ugh, why won't you fit," Myra said as she yanked on my wires, sending small, electric shots to the parts of me they controlled. I tried my best to withstand the pain, for Myra, but when my sensors shut off, she knew something was wrong.

"Sorry you keep malfunctioning, buddy. Don't worry, I'll get you fixed up soon."

Fix me? What happened to being "perfect?" How had I fallen from that? What if I remained imperfect forever?

"Myra!" the female human voice yelled again, louder than before.

I didn't see Myra's reaction as a large backpack, covered in pins and buttons from the different science fairs Myra attended, opened and scooped me up.

Several hours later, I'm still in the backpack, peering through the loose seams, when the sound of a small, female human approached. I watched her grab my human's wrist and drag her over to a table, laughing. They talked over lunch, giggling and sharing stories and superstitions.

She was tall for a small human, with long, flat brown hair that shook as she jumped up and gestured wildly. Her green eyes were complemented by her wacky outfit, adorned with handmade jewelry and a hand-sewn, nature-themed jacket that Myra later described as "cool." Myra mentioned her name, but to me, she would always be 'Other Human.' At some point in the conversation, my name popped up.

"What's a Cypher?" Other Human asked.

Carefully, Myra reached into her bag and pulled me out. I sat up straight, grinning internally when Other Human gasped.

"You have a robot!" Other Human said loud enough to draw annoyed glances from nearby tables.

"Shh," Myra said, laughing slightly. "I finished building him last night. Well mostly... still a few kinks I need to work out."

Other Human's eyes grew wide, followed by the biggest grin I'd ever seen. "That's so cool! You're like Tony Stark level genius."

Myra's cheeks turned bright red, and her pupils dilated. The sight made my electronics warm again, despite nothing happening to make them overheat. I thought back to last night, Myra's tears, and my helplessness. If this other human made Myra happy, then I could live with that.

So, I did. For the next twenty years, Other Human followed us everywhere, through every triumph and letdown. They went to the same high school and kept in contact from separate colleges, internships, and jobs. They stayed close, always sharing lunch before embarking on new projects or life chapters, as was tradition.

Today, we hosted lunch at our house and Other Human was already here. Good. Maybe she could talk some sense. Myra, my Myra, wanted to sell me; and I didn't have the mechanical capability to talk, besides a few pre-recorded phrases that wouldn't do my protest justice. We entered, Myra walking with her impossibly long legs and me rolling at her side. I utilized one of the few upgrades I liked: a screen broadcasting my perpetual scowl.

We passed through the basement robot-charging center first, a place I once dreaded but now longed for. I didn't know how lucky I was before: never imagining Myra would get rid of me, my only job to keep her company in the workshop and tolerate Other Human.

The basement was cold, particularly on the concrete, factory-style floors. Identical gray robots with numbers on their heads sat in rows, plugged into their charging stations. They stared blankly at me, like always, confusion spreading across their mechanical, screen faces. Myra didn't notice, which was good. She would've reprogrammed them, assuring they displayed the happy, smiling faces customers expected.

It was unnecessary, of course. Her new creations only felt the need to be efficient and were confused by others who didn't share that objective, like me. Initially, I felt pity, but soon realized the advantage. An emotional robot was an inefficient one and an inefficient robot was useless.

Their appearance was unchanging, except the numbers on their metal heads, always identifying the most efficient robot at any given moment. Upon closer inspection, the number one robot stood about a centimeter taller than the rest.

"Come on, Cypher," Myra said, clicking a remote I pretended controlled me. She was at the top of the steps, about to enter the kitchen, when I rolled up the ramp built next to the steps.

Other Human waited at the top. It still surprised me how big they'd grown. Both were taller, obviously, Myra in a dark purple suit and Other Human in a green and silver, self-designed dress. Their eyes were the same, minus the ever-growing dark lines underneath them. Other Human tried to cover them up with makeup, but Myra let them grow.

Other Human turned and strutted over to us in her giant high heels.

"Thank you for coming." Myra pulled Other Human into a hug.

"Of course! These lunches are always a good time: you spout off some crazy idea; I recommend you get some professional help; then you do it anyway," Other Human said.

Not completely true. Occasionally, Other Human had the crazy idea, or she would agree with Myra's, or Myra would take her advice and back down. I hoped she held the same power over this decision and agreed with me.

"All right, let's get straight to the point. Why are you selling Cypher? He's practically family," Other Human asked, always blunt.

Myra blinked, her eyebrows narrowing, then laughed nervously. She took a step back, away from both of us. "I thought you were willing to help me..."

"This is me helping you."

Other Human approached her. "Well?"

"The world deserves to see him," Myra said.

I didn't want the world to see me, only Myra. Other Human crossed her arms and raised an eyebrow. I tried to do the same, adjusting my digital face and placing my metal arms on top of each other accordingly.

Myra closed her eyes and wrapped her arms around herself. "I built Cypher in the corner of my parents' cold, messy garage, right after my grandma died," Myra said. "I look at him and remember tears streaming down my face, the ones I had to blink away to see what I was building. Then, I believed he was alive for the majority of my childhood, not some sort of malfunctioning hunk of metal. I was delusional and thought Cypher was some sort of friend, I just... want to move past that time of my life. At thirty, isn't it time?"

Every part inside me broke. Energy drained out of me as if someone forgot to change my battery. I was only a reminder of a bad memory. Why couldn't she see I was around for the good ones too? Other Human pulled her into a hug, something I couldn't do.

"You and your corners. You always start out in one... as a student everyone overlooks or an engineer nobody listens to," Other Human said. "You always get out. I pulled you out of one at school, and you pulled yourself out of one at work. Now you're the owner of a major tech business. You can boss everyone else around."

Myra pushed herself out of the hug and grabbed the remote and a sandwich. "Well, maybe Cypher shouldn't be in one either. This is best for both of us, and if you won't help, then I'll do it myself."

Myra offered a strained smile as she took me out of the box and placed me on the floor. "He's a good robot. You'll be happy with him. Here's the remote."

I was in shock. Myra was selling me to a customer. I would clean cars for the rest of my life in this old, wealthy human's garage. The garage, the place Myra was so keen to forget? She would lock me in there forever.

"All right, whatever. I'll let you know if I have to return him. Now leave," the old human ordered. Myra nodded and backed away toward the door.

Wait, I didn't say goodbye. She was leaving already.

Pale arms lifted me up, then wavered, almost dropping me. The old human was taking me away... forever.

"Its face keeps changing from angry to sad to confused, and wait, now its tires are moving," the shrill human said.

"Cypher does that sometimes. Don't worry, he'll stop eventually. Just press the smiley face button," Myra said, still drifting toward the door, farther and farther away from me.

The shrill human clicked the remote repeatedly, but the order fell mute on my distressed robot brain. Myra touched the doorknob of the door leading out and I lost it. My gears squealed, louder than ever before, until probably everyone in the world heard.

The shrill human dropped me and covered her ears. Myra did the same at the door. Only when she let go of the door handle did I stop. For a moment everyone was silent, staring at me in horror. The shrill human was the first to speak, slowly and deliberately. "Get it out."

"Ma'am, I can fix him," Myra said weakly.

The shrill woman shoved me into her arms and grabbed a remote from the couch, holding it like a dagger. She chased us out of the house.

"GET IT OUT!" She slammed the pristine, white door in our faces.

Myra didn't look at me as we headed to the car, didn't look at me the entire ride home, nor did she look at me when we finally reached her house. She left me downstairs in the basement, but I followed her. She didn't care.

We sat in the kitchen for hours, me staring up at Myra and Myra staring out the window.

Ring! Ring!

Myra's phone tried to get her attention. At least one piece of tech around here was good at their job. She picked it up and held it to her ear. Her face fell and tears streamed down her face. I only heard a sentence as Myra dropped the phone absentmindedly, not caring when the screen cracked: Other Human-no-Lola was in a car accident on her way home from work. She didn't survive.

Despite never really caring for Lola, I drove into Myra's room to think. Bad choice. Myra's room was covered in photographs of the two of them. Lola and Myra having sleepovers, attending each other's graduations, traveling, celebrating achievements, having lunches. In those pictures, Myra's smile was brighter than ever. How did you make her so happy?

She didn't answer and I didn't expect one. That's when I noticed I was in the pictures too. How did I make her so happy?

By being there. A voice answered from the back of my head, the same voice as the old woman in Myra's videos, Myra's grandma. My eyes locked on an old, handwoven basket shoved into the corner of Myra's room. I rolled to it and brought it to Myra with my robotic arms.

She huddled in the corner of the kitchen, next to the disassembled kitchen appliances, crying into her knees. She lifted her head when I dropped the basket in front of her. Her dark brown hair was messy, and her chocolate eyes were bloodshot. Almost like the day she made me, the day I came alive. I pointed to the stitched inscription on the front:

To make the heavy loads lighter.

Love,

Grandma

Myra pulled me into a hug, the first in years. She stared at the basket, then at me, her forehead wrinkled, and her eyebrows knitted together.

"You're alive?"

Hanging Rock

POTTED LILLIES

BY GEORGE LIES

"Potted lilies" is what Tommy Flanagan heard from his beau Monica as she pulled back from him in her quiet sort of way. She stared at the front window logo of Rustic Garden shop, and then pushed open the door. "I'll be a moment."

Enjoying a cool June in Pittsburgh, away from summer's humidity, they had been strolling Walnut Street through the chic Shady Side neighborhood, home to brand name shops like Green Leaf Vegan, Mud House Coffee, and Victoria's Secret. He plopped himself on an outside bench and felt redeemed that his mother approved of his new girl. He scanned the street: a smug lady in red held a white poodle; giggling teenagers held a reflective shiny vintage bag; a tuxedoed man fixed his string tie in the front seat of a Ferrari at curbside.

He almost felt out of place. Not a single familiar face from his late nights of hanging out, except—except for that woman with a slight build crossing Walnut Street and urging a cheap baby stroller through traffic as drivers braked and waved her on.

Tommy hoped she didn't see him. What was her name? Two years prior they had drifted apart after a few disastrous nights of drinking. What's-her-name now looked out of place in the chic neighborhood: a smudge on her cheek, torn jeans, and stringy hair. She had worked as a nurse at a local hospital, he remembered, and spent weekends cleaning her apartment. She hated dirt, as he learned, but she drank liquor heavily as she enjoyed flirting at local taverns in Oakland.

Tommy kept on guessing at her name. He resorted to a mind game that a buddy taught him when he worked at a convenience store before landing a salesclerk job at Macy's downtown. Go through the alphabet, his friend advised, and sound out names by letters.

He got to G but no obvious names fit what's-her-name who, he recalled, enjoyed lounging half-naked on a cold concrete porch landing outside her apartment. She'd stare at a dark sky full of stars, her head on a pillow, her body wrapped in a heavy blue hospital blanket.

He skipped letters H and I and got to J, recalling a few old names—Jessica, no; Jennifer, no; Jackie, no. He thought of K for Karen, no.

A bunch of honking cars on Walnut Street disrupted Tommy's name game at the letter L—at the same time that what's-her-name passed blindly between cars. She hitched the stroller wheels up and onto the sidewalk, barely twelve feet from Tommy on the bench.

She started off in the opposite direction only to pause at a hardware store on the corner. Leaning over, she tied the stroller straps to a wooden bench against the wall and pulled open the door, the tingle of a tiny bell startling her. Tommy stayed put on the bench. Not Meranda, no, and surely not Teresa, as in Mother Teresa. Tommy glanced at his letter M—Monica inside the flower shop. He lit a cigarette. He considered the blue stroller parked on the sidewalk but the first drag of smoke gave him a rush, spinning his mind to their last date.

—◆○◆—

They had driven to South Side, a neighborhood once known for steel mills and bars full of steelworkers. They attended a novo arts exhibit in a third-floor loft over an old theater. He helped with her jean jacket, unveiling a flowery blouse, and noticed his mother sipping a glass of red wine. She took him aside. "Where'd you find that one? She's pale—all skin and bones. What, she don't like corn beef and cabbage?"

"She's okay," he said. "Works at a hospital."

"A nurse, eh? Back when you came visiting me, when I was sick at the hospital," she said, "you disappeared on me as soon as a nurse came in, attending to a sick girl in the next bed."

"I can't stay long," Tommy said. "We've got plans tonight."

His mother's eyes narrowed as she sipped her wine. In the adjacent room, what's-her-name laughed out loud at a comment from a visiting older artist of classical nude painting. "Just you mind your P's and Q's," his mother said as she moved to the bar table of the reception. "We don't want any little ones with blue eyes running around—now do we?"

What's-her-name wrapped up her chat with the older artist; she nodded and gave him a goodbye hug. She grabbed her jacket, ready to leave.

Tommy drove them in his old Plymouth Chevy over the bridge spanning the Monongahela River to the Decade Lounge. Tommy started in on cuba libres of Bacardi 151 rum and coke while what's-her-name drank draft beer and shots of Smirnoff vodka. Their intake of rum and vodka, he recalled, injected an edge into the night. He expected the worst.

At midnight, she began dancing, first with the Decade bar owner, then his frisky twenty-something son. Tommy headed barside where he laid his head on the counter until he felt droplets in his face. She had come back, dipping her hand in a warm draft beer and sprinkling him awake. "I'm going to be busy," she said. "Go on home to your mother. Call me later."

She picked up her purse and walked out of the lounge, the bar owner's son on her arm.

⋯⋯⋯⋯⋯❖⋯⋯⋯⋯⋯

While waiting on Monica in the flower shop, Tommy Flanagan searched through the alphabet, testing names. He had gotten to N, O and P but skipped Q, and came to the letter R. No luck, no name came to mind. When he drew on his cigarette, an ember stung his finger. He stubbed the butt in a dirt bucket when Monica came out of the garden shop. She held two flowerpots: a small one holding budded lilies; the other, a large pot displaying long stemmed large green leaves.

"Grab this one, will you please?" She handed him the pot holding five-foot tall leaves. "Aren't these great? The lilies will open in a few days. I'll put the big pot on my parents' front porch or maybe in their living room. Or would your mother like that one?"

Behind the green leaves, Tommy only heard Monica's words as he grappled with the pot up against his summer jacket. He peeked around the pot of stems in his palms. Monica held one plant against her round face; the potted lilies in her arms seemed like a pearl necklace framed by her bobby cut hair and green sweater. "Whatever you say." Tommy began walking away from the nearby corner.

"Where you going?" she asked. "The car's that way."

"Distance is about the same."

"Let's go to that corner," she said. "Turn down the alley to the lot."

A breeze caught the leaves, and the pot skewed off balance in Tommy's arms. He recovered and shuffled along the sidewalk, following Monica's reveling in finding potted lilies. Before turning into the alley, she paused at the hardware store on the corner near the blue baby stroller outside. Monica scoured the street, before addressing Tommy with the question: why did someone leave a baby on the sidewalk?

"This pot is getting heavy," Tommy said.

"Why on earth—?" Monica put her hand to her chin. "Why leave a baby alone?"

"None of our business."

"It is our business."

The tiny bell tinkled when the shop door opened and what's-her-name came out onto the sidewalk. She placed a brown paper bag in the stroller's rear pocket netting then noticed Monica staring at the baby. "Oh, sister, I know what you're thinking—someone left a baby here," she said. "I know exactly what I'm doing."

"I wondered if—"

"If little baby's left abandoned—right?" She crooked her arm on her hip.

"I'm so sorry, I thought—" Monica blushed as she glanced back at Tommy behind the pot of large green leaves. Then she handed off the other pot to him, too.

"You can bet your ass, honey—I'm not losing this baby to no one." She angled the stroller toward Monica. "Want a look-see?"

"She's a beauty." Monica gazed into the stroller. "Lovely blue eyes."

"Her father's eyes. Well, I'm not sure who—get my meaning? I dropped that chump before I knew this one was on the way. Might be another's."

"I see."

"I do have my ways with men—like you do, I see."

"How sweet of you to say that."

"Pretty lilies you have there." She freed the stroller from its tether to the bench. "Today I'm cleaning house and needed cleanser and window wash. It's a real bitch."

"We have to go." Monica deliberately stepped back to the pot of large leaves hiding Tommy and then kept on going down the alley.

What's-her-name caught sight of the green plant that camouflaged Tommy. "You better keep on your toes with that one. Dot your I's and cross your T's—if you want to keep her pleased."

He didn't say a word as he began treading backwards into the alley. A gust of wind fluttered the large green leaves and Tommy grappled with the second pot of lilies. He turned toward the alley parking lot only after he saw what's-her-name crossing back over Walnut Street. He caught up to Monica at the open car door.

"That woman's young, and so frail," Monica said. "She does everything alone—like cleaning house and raising a baby—so fragile like lilies."

"That's life, I'm sure she gets by," Tommy said. "Buckle up."

Before getting into the car, he came to the next letter of the alphabet game. He ignored the letter T, for he knew Teresa didn't fit, and surely not Mother Teresa. He jumped to S when he recalled a TV show about a witch named Samantha.

"I didn't catch her name." Monica closed her passenger door. "Wonder how she lives and what she does without the baby's father around?"

Tommy backed the car out of the parking space and hit the turn signal. He still had to traverse Walnut Street and dropped letters U through Z. He never looked back until he realized he skipped the letter L, for Lilly.

THE BUCKET OF BLOOD

By Geoffrey C. Fuller and S. James McLaughlin

Verna sits in the booth by the jukebox. Her bony hands straighten the rumples in her skirt and blouse before patting her graying dark hair. Her face is pale as she stares vacantly at a beer bottle on the table. She's just gotten off her shift here at Wright's Tavern. Instead of heading home on this All Saints Day, she plopped herself in the empty booth to sip a cold Schlitz to pass the time.

"He's gone, Verna." Owner Red West, standing next to her table, cranes his head toward the door. He turns back to her, his eyes lingering slightly on her powdered black eye. "Why don't you stay a while? You don't have to go home to that."

"He'll be back. He wants me to fix his supper." She slides her finger down the bottle between the edges of the label leaving a glassy, brown trail in the condensation. "I told him to get his wife to do it and leave me the hell alone."

"He shoved you pretty hard. You okay?"

Vera lightly massages her smarting arm. She's sure that by the next day, a deep purple bruise would blossom. "I'm fine. Henry pulled him off me." She gives a half smirk, glancing at the drunken garbage collector who's resumed drinking at the bar. "Good thing you opted not to let the cops take him outta here or Bill would have drug me out that door by my hair."

Red lets out a resigned whistle. "He gave ol' Bill a sweet smooch on the face, didn't he?"

"He'll be back. You know it, I know it." Verna slumps lower in her seat.

"Well, he oughtta be too embarrassed. Betty and I'll make sure you get home safe."

The next hour goes by slowly. By the time the yellow cab pulls up outside, the bar is louder and busier, and no one notices Bill peering through the glass of the door. In the booth across from Verna, Red and Betty now sit, listening to Henry as he stands, slightly swaying and very intoxicated, between their table and Verna's. All four of them turn their heads when they hear a bellow.

"Who was the son of a bitch that hit me?" yells Hacker.

"I was," Henry says over the new quiet. "What are you going to do about it?" He squashes his cigarette in the ashtray on Red's table and straightens his shoulders. "I'll hit you again."

"Oh, no, you won't!" Bill edges closer until he's a few feet from Henry. His gnarled hand jerks out of his gray topcoat; patrons gasp and mutter as they spot his pistol. A young waitress ducks under the counter. Verna presses herself against the wall of the booth.

Bill points the Walther P38 at Henry, his arthritic finger on the trigger. It almost looks like a toy gun, the kind that shoots a "Bang!" flag.

"You won't hit anybody again!"

The loud pop from the gun is not toy-like and sends the entire room into a panic. Screams and scuffles erupt as Henry falls to the floor.

Verna's hands protectively fly out as though she's trying to push him away. "Please!" she screams. "Please, Bill! Don't shoot me!"

He regards her angrily, squeezes the trigger once more. The bullet zips between her fingers, jerking her head back as it cracks a hole above the center of her left eye and bursts out just above her left ear and lodges in the wall with a wet stamp of warm spray. Her head bounces off the booth, falls face-first onto the table. A quarter-sized hole oozes red chunky blood as the door swings closed behind Bill Hacker.

"Bucket of Blood" first appeared in the true crime, *The WVU Coed Murders: Who Killed Mared and Karen?* and reveals an earlier murder in the life of a person of interest, William Bernard Hacker.

FAMILY BUSINESS

By Melissa Reynolds

William Conner pulled his mount to a stop and wiped sweat off his forehead. He slapped his hat against his leg, knocking the dirt off, sending little puffs of dust floating in the still air. Storm a-comin'. Guaranteed. The heat would bring one heck of a thunderstorm. He'd been running wagon trains out west long enough to know the warning signs. Best to stop a couple hours early near Strant Canyon.

He kept an eye on the heavy-laden wagons which tended to tilt dangerously when turning onto Hadonn Trail. The last of the wagon train lumbered by with wheels creaking. Today was Peter Galloway's turn to bring up the rear and judging by the sour look on his face, they'd be hearing his complaints about dust choking up his lungs and those of his oxen all night. If the damn fool would just wear his bandana like the rest of the sensible folk, he'd have less to bellyache about.

Peter shouted for his wife, Emily, to get him a drink and when she didn't respond fast enough, he hollered curses. William bit his tongue. He didn't have a wife and wasn't one to talk, but common sense told him that a good man who treated his family decent-like wouldn't have daughters who cowered like Peter's did. Shame about the Galloway girls, but he couldn't do anything for them. His job was to get them safely across the prairie and nothing more.

The afternoon passed in a slow hazy cloud. When they reached Strant Canyon, he gave the signal to circle the wagons. Peter jumped down from his buckboard the instant his wagon rolled to a stop and marched over.

"Why are we stopping right now? We still have a couple good hours left. We could go at least four more miles."

"Storm's a-comin', Mister Galloway. Don't want to get caught in the open round these parts."

Peter pointed skyward. "There's no clouds."

"No, sir." William led his horse to a patch of grass to hobble him for the night. "But Injuns won't take too kindly to us stopping on their hunting grounds this time of year either." William began unsaddling his horse. He always pulled out the Injun card to scare the hard to deal with folks into doing what he wanted—and it usually worked—but Peter wasn't buying.

"I'd imagine that this far out, every area we stop will make some Savage mad." Peter scowled at him. "You're just lazy."

William shrugged and turned back to brushing down his horse. Peter stomped off and yelled at his family. The other folk barely paused in their chores. Small cooking fires sprang up and the men unhitched their oxen, but Peter continued harassing his family, ignoring his oxen team who restlessly stamped. The eldest daughter, Sara, said something and Peter backhanded her. She cradled her cheek, and her mother rushed to her side.

William moved closer as Sara wheeled and ran off. Peter made to chase after her, but William stopped him. "Listen here, your oxen need a-tendin'. Why don't you see to them and cool your heels?"

"And why don't you mind your own damn business?" Peter squared off with William, ready to fight.

William lowered his voice so only Peter could hear. "You finally ready to take on someone your own size?"

Peter sputtered and his face turned a mottled shade of red.

"That's what I thought. Go see to your team."

Emily edged toward the back of their wagon. "Pete, why don't I fix you your favorite supper?"

Peter glared at her a moment and with one final glance in the direction Sara had gone, he turned to his oxen. Emily disappeared behind the wagon and the younger girls tumbled out, the youngest whining and crying.

Two hours passed and Sara still hadn't returned. The storm he'd promised was cresting the horizon. William normally wouldn't have worried about Sara, many of the settlers disappeared for hours at a time to hunt, but under the circumstances he couldn't relax. So he left his dinner and causally headed in the direction she had gone. He found her practicing with her family's rifle. He watched for a while admiring her shooting.

He made some noise so as not to startle her then said, "You've got a sharp eye there, miss."

She reloaded the rifle and aimed it at William.

"I don't mean no harm."

"No, but he does." Her calm face was pale.

William turned slowly, half expecting to see Injun warriors lined up behind him. Instead, he saw Peter.

"Stop right there," Sara said coldly.

"You listen here you worthless whore, I'm tired of your antics. You have your mother worried sick. Get your behind back to the wagon before I tan it."

William moved out of the line of fire. "Let's not do anything rash—"

"Oh, you mean like he's done to me and my sisters our whole lives? Or how about last night when he crawled up next to me?" She cocked the gun and leveled it at Peter's chest. "You have no right to call me a whore when you're the monster who made me one."

William stared at Peter in shock. He knew the man was bad news, but he hadn't suspected this.

"That's family business and you'll not to go running your mouth about it!" Peter lunged forward and the gun went off. Peter fell and lay still.

William moved closer to Sara, slowly as he would with a wild horse. Her body shook and tears streamed down her face. In the most soothing voice he could muster he said, "It was an accident. A horrible accident, right?"

She shook her head, and he grabbed the rifle. "C'mon miss. Storm's a-comin'."

Sara collapsed against him. "What have I done?"

William moved her away from Peter's body and toward camp. "You were just handlin' family business."

JUNK FOOD

By Jane Ellen Freeman

A low hum vibrated at the edge of the vast state forest accompanied by a pulsing meld of green and yellow. Within seconds, the colors faded to a muted blue, then winked out, and the hum softened to a barely detectable murmur. A lone owl hooted once, twice, before the night returned to silence. A deer lifted her head, stepped back as if to run, then resumed browsing. No humans saw the small ovoid ship resting in a circle of junipers.

Sonny pulled his battered Jeep between two fir trees at the end of the fire access road.

"Thank Jesus. I hit my head when you flew over that last bump." Pats shivered and wrapped her arms around her body. She'd selected her outfit for the drive-in, not a forest hike to who-knows-where. Her cropped tank top trimmed with tattered lace offered little coverage and no warmth to the exposed flesh above her denim cutoffs. "You said you had something special to show me. This ain't it, I hope."

"Nah, stop your fussin'. Here, put this on." He reached behind her seat and handed her his workout sweatshirt.

"Ugh. Stinks." Pats glared and held the shirt at arm's length.

"Just manly drips, darlin'. I been saving another kind for you."

Pats giggled. Making out it in the woods would be different, better than straddling Sonny and bumping her thighs on the gear shift and door handle. She pulled the sweatshirt over her head and grabbed the grocery bag with the cheese twists and Red Vines—the stringlike licorice she loved playing with more than eating. Maybe she'd tie Sonny up with the long licorice strands and then nibble him free. He liked that kind of thing. A warm feeling crept from under her belly and flushed her chest and face.

Sonny noticed. "Hey, Babe, wait for me." He paused and gave Pats his sexy up and down look. "Unless you want to get started now?"

Pats shook off his hand that had started to grope her chest. "Just thinking about it, hot stuff." She shook her head. "Nah, I'll wait."

Sonny lifted his backpack from behind his seat, and he and Pats climbed out of the Jeep.

"Look what I got." He unzipped the pack so Pats could see. Under the blanket was a bottle of peach-flavored Boone's and those sticky raspberry cakes Pats loved. She stood on tiptoes and nibbled his ear.

"Yum," she cooed. "Let's go."

The forest seemed unusually dark though it was just past eight o'clock. With his back to the fir trees and his Jeep, Sonny peered behind a stand of giant rhododendrons.

"Shit. Where is it?" He pulled back an overhanging branch. "There. It's overgrown some, but I found it."

They took three steps on the deer path past the huge shrub when Sonny's flashlight dimmed, then went out.

"Double shit." He smacked it against his palm and the light obliged, once again revealing the narrow trail. Pats leaned into him, her arm around his waist. They both tripped on a tree root.

Sonny wriggled out of Pats's hug. "Too hard to walk all tangled up."

She stopped and punched his arm. "I'm ready to go back. Can't walk in these flipflops. Let's go to the drive-in like we planned. I wanted to see that Black Lagoon mov--"

Sonny put his arms around her and kissed her mouth mid-whine.

"Ummm, mint gum." Pats lifted her face for another kiss.

"I'll share." Sonny laughed. This time he pushed his gum into her mouth with his kiss.

"Gross." But instead of spitting out the gum, Pats began to chew.

A few stumbles later, the trail curved around another patch of rhododendrons circling a weeping willow leaning over a rocky stream bed.

"Look. Straight ahead, near that willow." The flashlight beam revealed the outline of a cabin. It had no porch, but two slabs of wide stone stepped up to a weathered door.

"Spooky," Pats whispered. "Sonny, is this it?"

"Hush. You'll love it. Private. With a bed."

Pats cowered behind him as Sonny pushed open the creaking door. Inside, a wobbly table flanked by two equally unstable chairs crowded the center of the room. Next to one wall stood a bed, not quite a double, but wider than a cot. A shelf held what looked like a scout's mess kit along with two red Solo cups wrapped in plastic.

Now that they were in, and nothing scary scurried around, Pats began to relax. She opened a shallow box next to a tin holder. "Goody. Candles. How'd you know all this was here?"

"Pops and I used to hunt squirrels and such. We stayed here many a time. Never got too many squirrels, but Pops liked to smoke and drink, and Gran was dead set against either."

Sonny lit one of the candles with his Bic. Pats sat on the bed and patted the space beside her. "Better than the Jeep, that's for sure. More comfy than the ground too."

Before joining her on the bed, Sonny yanked the blanket out of his pack, tossed it to her, and poured the Boone's into the cups.

"A toast," he said, settling down beside Pats. "To privacy."

They touched the cups together, then each took a long drink. Sonny set their Solos on the table and pulled the sweatshirt over Pats's head. "Let's see them tits."

Pats slipped the tank top over her head and ran her tongue lightly over her lips. "Might get cold," she whispered.

Sonny's shirt and jeans were already on the floor. He reached behind Pats and undid her bra. He grinned. He liked this one. All silky, black and sexy, trimmed with lace. He pushed Pats back on the blanket. "I'll warm you up, darlin'."

※

The cabin had only one window, but it was enough to let the soft candlelight out into the forest. Unhampered with mechanical lighting, two creatures moved toward the light, their footsteps stealthy and soundless on the damp carpet of leaves. The taller of the two pointed to the sliver of light under the cabin's door.

The other touched its companion on its gnarly shoulder and blinked huge, purplish eyes. Round bulbous appendages rose like Mickey Mouse ears from the top of each of their heads. Waving a thin arm, the shorter alien gestured toward the window.

They stared through the dirt-smeared glass into the structure's interior. The taller being lifted its hand and, using the pad of its longest digit, rubbed a clean circle on the glass. Gasping, it stepped back, and held its middle, a low gurgle erupting from its throat. The shorter one put a purple eye close to the glass. The alien also inhaled abruptly, moved away from the window, and bending over, emitted the same gurgling burst of sound. The two slipped behind a tree, shoved into each other, and not nearly as quiet as their footsteps, bumped and pushed, all the time grunting and panting and clicking their sharp pointed teeth.

⸺◦⸺

Pats moaned in that low, throaty way Sonny loved. He pushed deeper. She was close. His climax exploded at the same time she lifted her hips and shuddered. He lowered over her, still keeping his weight on his arms. Sounds outside drifted into Sonny's consciousness. An animal? Racoon? He looked toward the window. His eyes riveted to a clean circle on the filthy glass.

"Pats, someone's out there. They looked in," Sonny whispered, his voice hoarse. He eased his body off Pats, his motions slow and silent.

Gurgles. Clicks. Closer? They both stared at the door.

Again, as if slow, quiet movements would forestall what was on the other side of the flimsy door, he picked up Pats' shorts and his sweatshirt.

Hands trembling, she pulled on her shorts and the sweatshirt and stepped into her flipflops. Sonny had on his shoes and jeans, his shirt in his hands. The door creaked and opened, first an inch, then more, then a hard push flung it wide. The door complained with a screech as it teetered on a rusty hinge. Two creatures from the stuff of nightmares and B-list horror films blocked the opening. Both were taller than any human but thinner and with a phosphorous-like skin.

The taller alien moved forward, its slender arms reaching out toward Pats. She opened her mouth to scream but her throat closed, frozen in terror. Backing toward the bed, she fell back and sat down hard. The bag of cheese twists rustled noisily beside her. Sonny grabbed the bottle from the table and raised it like a club.

"Stop," Sonny demanded. His shout wavered as he also backed up to the bed.

The aliens paused, their purple eyes gleaming. The tall one sniffed loudly and reached out again. Pats whimpered and moved farther back toward the cabin wall. The shorter alien picked up several strands of the licorice candy from the table, smelled them, snorted, and wrapped the rope-like candy around its wrist. It looked at its companion, and its forked tongue ran over its thin lips. The other alien moved its head up and down, made a soft, gurgling sound, bent over, and clutched its middle. Then it reached toward the bed. Pats swallowed her second try at a scream and thrust the bag of cheese twists in front of her.

Clicking and growling back in his throat, the alien grabbed the bag, spilling cheese twists over the cabin floor. Both crouched on all fours, gobbling and huffing.

"Pats, go." Sonny's whisper caught in his throat. "Slow." He set the wine bottle on the table, grabbed the flashlight, and pulled Pats in front of him and out the door.

They ran, hand in hand, the flashlight's beam boomeranging from trail to the crowding shrubs.

Pats fell, jostling Sonny. He dropped the flashlight which, of course, had had enough. It went out. Permanently this time.

"Triple shit, fuck." Sonny again smacked the light as if a severe beating would coerce it into cooperation.

Pats turned, her eyes seeking the candlelight spilling out of the cabin door. She wailed, "Sonnyyyyy, Look."

Backlit by the open door, the two creatures stood on the stone steps, their phosphorescent skin aglow. One pointed a long bony hand toward Sonny and Pats.

"Get behind that tree," Sonny whispered, groping in his pocket for his Bic. "Don't make a sound." As he watched, the two aliens seemed to argue, the small one pushing the taller one back into the cabin. After a long moment, Sonny flicked his lighter on. Tears streaked down Pats' face, and her eyes were wide with fear.

"Drive-in?" Sonny asked, kissing her lightly on her forehead.

Pats whispered, "Yes." She took Sonny's hand. "But not that Black Lagoon movie. Something funny."

———◦———

Air from the door made the candle's flickering light throw dancing shadows across the walls. The two aliens bounced around on the bed, gurgling and clicking and taking turns swigging the strange liquid from the bottle. When their coupling had finally quieted, the taller alien rolled off its partner, stood, and picked up a smooth piece of fabric from the floor. The alien, Urgah, sniffed, sneezed twice, and placed the shiny, black cloth on Plesor's head. The two cuplike sections fit perfectly over Plesor's receivers. Licking a smear of orange-yellow cheese from its thin mouth, Plesor popped a sticky sweet they'd found in the bag into its mouth and chewed. Hand in hand, the bag of cheese twists rustling in the otherwise silent woods, the two left the cabin. No human heard the growing hum from the ovoid ship. Nor did anyone see the lights glow from soft blue to rapidly pulsing green and yellow as the ship rose above the dense forest. At the cabin, the wax of the spent candle flooded the flame until it sputtered into darkness.

THE THINGS OUR OLD ONES TELL US

BY GWENYTH WINSHIP

My Irish grampy told me that a woman's song is a glimpse into her heart. What she sings, how she sings it, tells you all you need to know about who she is.

He shielded the side of his mouth as if imparting a great secret and glanced over surreptitiously at my grandmother. She didn't notice – was too busy waving her hands overhead, squawking at my mother, certainly not singing.

I think my grampy was wrong.

I don't believe the girls ('women' – 'females' – whatever they prefer) I've been with over the years have ever sung a song for themselves when we were together. I think they sing or play the song they want me to hear. Maybe they think it will strike a deeper chord. Maybe it is their last, hopeful resort to rally me into action. Maybe once or twice it almost worked – until I woke and found myself yanking my pants and sneakers back on.

Not sure. But I do wish my grampy was right. I wish I could say I've looked at a beautiful girl/ woman/ female, watched her sing, and had the epic realization that I was seeing deep into her core and wanted to...

I thought it happened once. Granted, I was out with my friends at a pub, and about one beer shy of being hammered. But it was St. Patrick's Day, the midnight hour felt young, jigs were loud, and bright, pearly whites flashing.

I ended up in a bar with a shamrock-sparkled door. One friend came in, probably to retrieve me. The lights were low, and folks were crowded about a dimly lit sound system. It must have been an Irish themed, slow-songs-only kind of night.

And time stopped.

The girl behind the microphone was a fucking angel.

I thought, right then and there, I could love you.

I'd never heard such a voice. I'd never felt such a feeling.

My friend pulled my arm – "Dude, let's go" – and I muttered back, "Shut up, I'm trying to listen."

When she finished, the lights brightened, her spell ended, and tall drinks or empty glasses clinked again. I walked straight to her. There's no point in not telling a gorgeous girl that she's gorgeous. She already knows it. She was seated with some friends – just fine, I'd meet her people.

But the first words out of her mouth shattered the teensy-tiny idea within me that maybe, just maybe, my grampy had been right.

She turned and looked at me. "Can I help you?"

I laughed, startled. "Uh – no. Yes. Can I have those extra napkins?"

It was the way she said it. The discomfort and disdain, so different from her music.

I shoved back to the bar, finding my regrouped friends.

What a dud, I either thought or said or hooted to the moon.

We ended up on the sidewalk again, piling out of the bar and ready to roll straight into the next adventure. But a girl stood outside. Different girl. Probably bad at singing, with brownish-blonde curls heaped in a ponytail, and a frown as she waited. Maybe for a ride.

She looked at me.

When our eyes met, her expression shifted into skeptical amusement. Her eyes were clearer, more knowing, than any person I'd ever met.

And that's when I learned the truth.

There's no such thing as falling in love with a girl who is just singing. But maybe there is such a thing as falling for one who sees through to your bones, the very second she lays eyes on you?

My Irish grampy didn't tell me the full story.

THE HAUNTING OF ERNEST JAMESON

BY ERIC CASDORPH

The house was quiet on the day the music changed. It was an old place, inherited from his parents, all peeling wallpaper and old wood, staircases just a bit too small for his feet like the clothes he'd grown up in. Hand-me-downs, like the house itself. He sat in the kitchen, staring out to the east at the rain coming through the clouds, painting long streaks along his mist-coated window.

He had nowhere to be. Ernest rarely did. He'd achieved that rarest of rares, though– he didn't owe a thing to any man alive. The rain pattered against the lake by the house, invisible fairy footsteps across the silvery water to where it emptied out into the river again.

He couldn't hear the rain, though. Not over Dana Fiume's music playing in his ear. She was a small artist years and years ago. When he thought of the past, he turned on "River Tune"– a song she'd recorded in his attic, just her and a guitar.

He knew every chord, ringing against the old mic like silverware on marble. He knew every breath, every slide of a guitar-string, every soft creak of the boards beneath her chair in the makeshift booth crowded with equipment.

He'd been there, after all. It was his attic. Belonged to his parents, at the time.

Ernest never had much talent for singing, found it better to speak rhythmically in the privacy of his own home, where folks couldn't be subjected to it unless they broke in, which he figured evened the deal out nicely– they picked a lock or broke a window, they got to suffer his voice.

The chorus was coming, and Ernest remembered their arguments– rivers had *banks*, not coasts, but she'd insisted it sounded better. In the end, he had to agree that she was right.

My love is like a river/ rolling, changing, shifting, shaping / the coast of our lives, raging and diving / and it's coming for you / just let it sweep you away.

He knew, right after the second chorus, a small creak came– Dana had almost fallen out of her chair on that one but kept the tape going. Good old Dana. Always there, at least in the music. It felt like part of her was still here, as long as he kept those recordings on his phone.

But then, the second chorus washed over him, and the creak came– a half-second too early. Ernest stopped, looking down at his phone. Two minutes, thirty-eight seconds. Didn't the creak come at thirty-nine? Was he losing his mind?

Ah, but too much of the song had passed now. He'd corrupted the experience, thinking about people gone. He looked out again at the rain coming down harsh, muddying the sandy lakeshore, and his face became something approximating gladness that he didn't have to go out in it.

His hands brushed across his brown mustache, adjusted his thick Buddy Holly spectacles, and he pulled the song back to the beginning and let the music wash over him again. The guitar, the songs, the chorus coming like a rolling wave.

My love is like a river/ rolling, changing, shifting, shaping/ the banks of
your
life/ raging and diving/ and it's coming for you/ just let it sweep you away...

This time, he recoiled. Those weren't the words. He knew every second of this song, had the measure of every measure. His headphones hit the table, the guitar rendered tinny by distance and cheap speakers as he turned his gaze to the rainy window.

There, where the steam of his tea met the mist of the glass, something was pushing itself against the hard and the clear. The rain– strong enough to wreck the local agriculture now– was falling around something out there, forming a half-shape. His eyes told him nothing was there; the rain told another story entirely.

Ernest ran. He scooped up his things smoother than he'd moved in years and hauled himself upstairs. The distance-harshened sound still played louder and louder from the headphones around his neck. He'd learned fear a long time ago, but this sat somewhere beyond that. The steps creaked with every movement, the house settling in the rain, as he bolted up them.

He'd had to be imagining it. What he wasn't imagining, though, was the way he put his foot down wrong, and a twinge of pain shot up his leg– the stair was too narrow, his muscles unstretched, and he'd pulled one. He swore, tea spilling onto the old rug and the mug chipping but kept moving to his bedroom.

He shut the door, clicked the old brass lock on a door made of older wood than him, a door that always dragged just a bit in the shutting. The music was still going, louder and louder now. He reached over and with a press of a button clicked his phone off and tossed it onto the floral-patterned comforter of the bed. In fact, he tossed it so hard the headphones disconnected and clattered off his neck directly onto the floor.

He turned to the old, varnished wardrobe, where some of his mother's old hippie feminist decorations still lay and opened it. He moved through clothes, fumbling until he found the familiar iron of a hunting rifle. His knuckles went white on the steel when he heard the door open.

Like the lock wasn't there. Like it had the key he kept around his neck and had let Dana borrow when she still associated with the living. He barely heard the creak of the woodhouse over the rain coming down.

He spun around, the rifle-barrel in his hands and the rest of the gun somewhere else in the closet, in need of repair. A shape stood in the flickering light of the hallway. He only saw it because of the way the rain and the leftover river it had maybe come out of played around its silhouette.

Slowly, inch by inch, he let his gaze turn, like the slightest move away from the figure might crack his spine—-to where the tinny, crackling noise of a phone's speakers was coming from. The thing had started to play again, without his touching it, the bridge to the last chorus.

It's coming for you/
It's coming for you/
It's coming for you/

The figure vanished between a flicker of light from the hall and stepped inside with him. In the dark room, he could barely see the figure itself, only its peculiar effect on the things around it. He had to fight past his fear to confer with his logic to understand exactly what was happening.

Five wet spots formed on the quilt, dragged themselves slowly into soft lines, playing around the outline of the embroidered cornflower, always Dana's favorite. She'd had the quilt made. It brushed over his phone's touchscreen, then moved on.

"Get away," he whispered, and the thing, whatever it was, gave no response. The door shut behind it, and Ernest realized how deeply the cold was working its way into his joints, smothering heat and choking warmth. Slowly, a handprint formed on the mirror, frost playing between finger-lines like ivy growing on brick.

The river-thing stepped closer, away from the window, and small slivers of ice crackled and fell to the floor where its feet landed. Still, the phone played, disjointed, skipping randomly along the song's timeline from the water on the screen.

It was standing above him now. He could tell by the dripping slush-water pooled at his socked feet, soaking into the wool. Something horrible occurred to him, then, as he looked out the window. From here, he had a perfect view of where the lake met the river– the exact spot where a riptide had

taken
Dana
under.

"It's you," he whispered, voice thick with...fear? Grief? He didn't know.

The rifle-barrel clattered to the floor. He wasn't going to hurt anyone with it anyway. Against his better judgment, with silvery chords of sharpness echoing through the room, his arms found the figure and his legs gave out. He didn't know what he expected, besides icy cold that clawed its way up his limb-nerves. He ignored it.

"You're here," he gasped, what few tears his body had turning to ice before they left his cheek. Every touch of this thing was a shock–no sign of movement, no cause, only effect. Something that might've been a hand cradled his cheek. He leaned into it. "Dana, I'm sorry," he whispered. "I should've– I should've been a better swimmer, I–"

Something like a railroad nail left in the freezer brushed his lips, quieting him, and the words were pulled from his lungs in icy-mist breath. The phone kept playing.

> *Just let go/*
> *Let go/*
> *Let go*

"I can't," he whispered. "Dana, I can't, because it was *my fault*. You're there, and I'm here, and it won't stop hurting."

Something hauled him upright, and the phone echoed again.

Changing/The coast of your life/Raging and diving

Something pulled on his wrist, gently, and he let it. Foot by foot, step by step, he walked downstairs. His phone was in his hand, though he didn't remember picking it up. Small steps creaked beneath wet socks, and he took his time, careful not to fall down the stairs.

The door opened to his touch. The rain was so much louder against the porch and the threshold. Ernest didn't bother to shut the door again, feeling the easy bend of old, good wood beneath his feet that gave way to mud, and after a minute, the riverbank, where the lake became rushing water again.

He looked out at the silver and the muck, and his phone played a final line before he dropped it to the ground.

Just let it sweep you away.

Here in the misty cold afternoon, the water looked like the shine of herring-scale or salmon-skin. Even in a storm, this place was kind in its beauty. It wasn't a bad spot. Not for this.

Ernest looked around for a silhouette and found none. "I'm sorry," he whispered to the air around him. "I'm coming."

Sometimes, the pain won. Sometimes it hurt too bad to let it sit inside and fester. Sometimes something killed you, and you just didn't know it. Ernest spread his arms, and let himself fall into the icy water, and

be

taken

under.

The cold was the first thing that hit him. Upon exposure he gasped, a deep, jagged thing that he had as much control over as he did his heartbeat or his blinking. It hurt, and immediately he spasmed in the dark and the wet, his body trying to eject water by any means necessary and finding only more.

This must've been how Dana felt, he thought, as the suffocation reached him, the animal panic. His hands scrabbled at the dirt-bank as he sank deeper, deeper, kicking wildly. Why was he flailing? This was what he wanted.

The last thing he thought, before the dark took him, was that maybe it wasn't.

Ernest awoke on the sandy shore of the lake, next to his phone, and immediately vomited water and bile onto the sand, body spasming. The downpour washed it away.

The phone had died. Water exposure. It lay there, silent and useless. He rubbed the back of his neck, icy-cold even in the rain. Felt like something had scruffed him the way grandma used to do to her cats.

"Just let go," he half-laughed. He left the phone there and began the walk back to his house, and barely felt the cold.

CURLING RIPPLES

TAKE ME OUT

BY ADAM HORNE

Gavrilo stared out the front window of the cafe and sipped his coffee. Brewed in the traditional Turkish fashion, he'd foregone adding cream or sugar. The strong, bitter taste suited his mood after their failure earlier in the afternoon. The plan had been simple; throw a bomb under the car as the motorcade left the airport.

He'd hidden amongst the crowds lining the route along with five other members of the Black Hand. He'd heard the explosion of a grenade going off before the car with their target went streaking past; the man wore full dress regalia and a cap with bright green feathers sticking out the top, his wife sitting beside him in a cream-colored dress. They both stared out the back of the convertible, moving too quickly for Gavrilo to risk taking a shot and giving away his position to the policemen swarming through the crowd.

He ran like a coward and hid in this cafe, waiting. Had any of the others made it out safely? An hour passed and he ordered a fresh pot when the waiter asked if he was ready for his check. He refilled his cup. He had no reason to believe the authorities followed him, but he'd taken a seat by the window to keep an eye out.

The sound of several engines came from down the street, and he craned his neck forward to see better. Although automobiles were becoming more common in Sarajevo, several of them together could mean trouble. He slouched down behind his table as they progressed towards the cafe and breathed a sigh of relief when it became apparent they weren't police.

The vehicles stopped at the intersection in front of the shop, and the one in the lead stalled its engine with a sputter. The driver tried to restart the machine with no luck. After the third try, a man in a military uniform exited the second car and climbed onto the running board of the first.

Inside the stalled vehicle sat a woman in a pale dress and a man wearing a cap with bright green feathers. He leaned across her to speak to the guard through the window.

Gavrilo jumped up from his table and rushed out the front door of the cafe. He reached under his shirt and gripped the pistol tucked into his waistband. When he was just over an arm's length from the side of the car, he pulled out the gun and fired through the open window.

The first shot struck his target in the side of the neck below the line of the collar. The woman turned toward her husband and gasped in shock, the blood spreading down the front of his uniform.

"Franz, for heaven's sake! What happened to you?" she asked.

His second shot went wide, striking her in the stomach. She lurched forward in surprise and collapsed on her husband's lap.

"Sophie, dear! Don't die! Stay alive for our children!" shouted the duke, who then slumped backwards against the seat.

Gavrilo pulled a small tin out of his pocket and opened it. He retrieved one of the capsules they'd bought from an arms dealer the week before. He bit down on it and the bitter taste of almonds filled his mouth, causing him to gag. He coughed and sputtered. Had he swallowed enough of the vile-tasting substance to do the job? To be certain, he raised the pistol to his own head.

Before he could pull the trigger, a guard tackled him and knocked the gun out of reach. The guard sat on Gavrilo's chest and pinned his arms to the ground so he couldn't move. Several men in uniform jumped out of the other cars and rushed to the one in the lead.

An older man with gray hair pushed through them, saying he was a doctor.

"Is your Imperial Highness suffering very badly?" asked one of the men.

"It is nothing." Despite the words, the duke's voice was weak.

The doctor frowned and pulled at the collar of the uniform as one of the guards worked frantically at the buttons. Although they disengaged, the shirt would not open.

"Get this damned thing off!" yelled the doctor. "I can't see the wound."

"The lapel has been sewn down," said the guard.

"You," said the doctor as he pointed to the driver of the second car. "There are scissors in my bag in the trunk of your car. Bring the whole thing."

The man nodded and rushed off. The doctor worked frantically to stop the bleeding, cutting away the jacket and undershirt after the driver returned with his tools. He pressed a handkerchief down to staunch the flow of blood and asked the duke how he was feeling.

"It is nothing," repeated the duke, but the end of his statement was punctuated with a rattle as he breathed out.

The look of worry deepened on the doctor's face. "Get this car started! We need to get Herr Ferdinand to the hospital!"

Gavrilo laughed at the men still running frantically about.

The guard on his chest glared down at him, pulled a fist back, and punched him in the eye. His head rebounded off the cobblestone pavement and stars filled his vision.

Before the blackness overtook him, he saw the duke take one final breath then stare glassy eyed into the distance.

I SPOKE TO THE WIND

By Andrei Nesterov

Everyone wants to have a comfortable life for themselves.

Victor's business, a language school in Moscow, went bankrupt after four years of struggle. He closed the office, brought piles of textbooks from the school to his apartment and, like a boxer who had been punched, was at a loss for a few days, not knowing what to do. He spent almost a week in his apartment, watching a crime series on his laptop.

Victor's mobile started ringing, reminding him about the real world, calling him to action. His former classmate, a woman from his native town, was phoning. Victor had gone to Yekaterinburg for university 150 miles away, then moved to Moscow in search of new opportunities.

"Hi sweetie, I hope you haven't forgotten about our class reunion in three days," the woman reminded him in a friendly voice with the local dialect where the letter "o" is emphasized. Victor felt a burst of energy. He switched off his laptop and started packing for the trip.

Before the day ended, he boarded the plane and was about to doze off when the man sitting next to him started to speak on the phone. "Yes, honey, I am on the plane...I'll see you in two days. No, I don't have a cold. I am in good health but thank you for asking."

It's touching when someone feels for you, Victor thought while the plane took off. Through the window, the lights of the city at night, white, orange, and yellow, were scattered on the ground beneath the aircraft, forming ornamental clusters and constellations.

Upon arrival at Yekaterinburg airport, the building, despite being recently renovated, looked lifeless. He remembered a different airport at the same site, overcrowded because airfare was low. People in the Soviet Union could easily afford to travel by air. Twenty-five years ago, some people had to stand as it was hard to get a seat. There were long lines in the cafeteria too, and the newsstands were sold out within an hour after the newspapers had been delivered. Victor ordered a taxi and hurried out of the airport.

Where are all these people going? Victor wondered as he walked out of the airport building, thinking how time could fly by so fast, taking away his years of youth. Was it really true that he was thirty-five now, and all alone?

Soon, he was on the train heading for his native town. In his carriage, the only passenger was an elderly woman who slept under blankets. Outside the window, coniferous woods alternated with fields. This view would stay here hundreds of years, unlike Victor and other people who spent their lives pursuing illusionary goals.

The train went past a ranger's house hidden among trees, and after passing a large lake, the train entered the town's outskirts composed of wooden cottages and five-story buildings. About a dozen passengers got off the train, mainly young girls and boys, probably students visiting relatives. Almost every newcomer was met by one person or several people. They walked to the parking lot together, excitedly chatting. Victor walked into the railway station which looked like a massive square-shaped aquarium due to floor-to-ceiling windows.

In an empty waiting room, Victor paused for a moment, admiring the drawing on the wall. It depicted three prominent figures from the town's history: a celebrated agronomist from the latter half of the 20th century, shown scattering wheat seeds from a basket tied to his waist with a white towel; a talented artist at his easel, capturing Italian people and landscapes from two centuries past; and a renowned sculptor from the 1930s, chiseling a masterpiece from a massive stone. This sculptor was famous for his statue of a topless woman with an oar, once displayed in numerous parks across the Soviet Union.

Victor exited the station and looked at the commemorative plaque on the corner of the building, honoring the policeman in 1994 stabbed by a fugitive there. Victor imagined that scene, went down the steps, entered the station square, took the only spare cab, and headed for the hotel.

The following day, he went to the reunion at an outdoor café. Russian and American music played, and former classmates walked around, greeting one another and chatting. A fraction of them continued to live in the town, while the others left for bigger cities.

The guy who shared a table with Victor, Alexei, was a newspaper reporter. In the 1990s, he was a local celebrity famous for articles exposing corruption in the town. He said in a sad tone, "today, reporters are only allowed to praise the local government and bosses and to write about gardening and pets. I am going to quit."

Another classmate, Anton, worked at the economic department of the local government. He gave Victor a hug and exclaimed, "I've heard that you do business, that's cool! We have few reliable people for our projects here. Come and work for us. A new sports center construction is coming to an end, a deputy manager for the center is required. A creative guy like you should give it some thought." Victor asked the old buddy to give him two or three days to think about it.

The woman who had called Victor to remind him about the reunion approached him and asked, "Have you heard that Yulya died? A terminal illness, nothing could help her."

Yulya had been his friend since childhood. He was drawn to her kindness. In junior school, they listened to fairytale records together. At one point, they went jogging most mornings, dreaming of becoming champions. When they grew older, they dated for a short time, had a few kisses, but then Victor left. Yulya graduated from school with an excellence award, went to college in the native town, had an unhappy affair with a married man. She ended up a single mother living in the town with her little son. Victor visited her once every few years when he came to see his relatives and friends.

"Where is her son Misha?" He had always liked the open-hearted boy who enjoyed making arts and crafts.

"In the orphanage. Yulya's parents passed away several years ago, and the other relatives were reluctant to adopt him."

The next morning Victor visited the orphanage on the town outskirts. Approaching the gate, he saw a group of kids walking in the yard, and there was Misha a little way aside from the others. The boy was uttering something quietly.

"Hi, Misha!"

The boy recognized Victor in an instant. "Hello, Uncle Victor!"

"What were you doing?" Victor asked.

"Speaking to the wind, so it stops breaking things. The wind broke the pinwheel I made."

"And how are you?"

"I am good, I got a diploma, for my drawings. I have another diploma, for the poem I wrote. I want to have a hundred diplomas!"

Victor listened to the boy and felt a new sense of purpose. "Misha, what are your dreams?"

"To fly into space and to discover a new star."

"Let's be good friends. I'll be visiting you a lot."

"Thank you, that's good," the boy answered.

Leaving the orphanage, Victor thought that he had found someone to live for. I'll adopt the boy and help him get through life, he thought. He took his mobile out of his pocket and dialed his classmate's number, "Hi, Anton, I agree to work on your projects."

Three months passed. One afternoon, Victor was walking with Misha in a park while chatting about the boy's day at school. The summer was ending, the ground in the park was covered with foliage of different colors, yellow, brown and crimson. A gust of wind picked up a fallen leaf and blew it up into the sky.

TEA FOR TWO

By Aimee Hoffer

The carriage dropped them in front of their destination, the steam horse tossing its head with a hiss and a screech. Thompson paid the cabbie and with a hiss and a clatter, the carriage pulled away, sunlight glinting off the brass studs of the steam-horse's neck, the back end behind the carriage belching smoke.

"Wretched things," the fair-haired Thompson muttered as he brushed soot off his arm, not noticing that his hair looked as if it had been sprinkled with pepper. "Ten years ago, they were the latest gadget and now they're all over London."

"Cheaper to use than actual horses," Wallace offered, thankful his own hair was black. "No feed, no stabling, and so on. Keep the street cleaner, too."

"Mm-hmm," Wallace said, pointedly brushing soot from his coat. He turned to look up at the frosting on the glass of the establishment in front of them, Sharpe's Tea Shoppe. "Let's hope Mr. Sharpe doesn't mind a little soot. You know what's riding on this."

"Oh, yes, Mr. Llewellyn was most emphatic." Wallace sighed. "He wants to take Sharpe's idea and open a chain of tea shops just like it all over the country—we only need to convince Mr. Sharpe to agree to sell."

Thompson swiped at his moustache and sighed when he spotted a smudge on his glove. "All right, let's get this over with. I'm dying for soap and hot water."

A brass plate next to the door stated, *Please Ring Bell and Enter,* so they did as instructed. Once they closed the door behind them, they found themselves standing on an ornamented iron grate and a blast of warm air hit them from above, neatly removing soot and dust from their coats.

With a hiss and a little geyser of steam, a curlicue coat rack dropped down the wall, and another brass plate above it invited them to hang their outer vestments. Once they had, another blast of air took care of any lingering soot, and an inner door swung open, showing them inside the shop.

"That's absolutely brilliant; the man's a genius," Thompson whispered with glee as they stepped inside. "Imagine having an entryway like that in every home!"

"I hear the idea was patented along with the tea shop," Wallace answered as a young hostess with red hair in a coil at the back of her head showed them to a table. "Whoever this Sharpe is, he's a canny businessman. We've our work cut out for us."

"Here you are, sirs," the young woman said as they took their seats. "Peruse the menu at your leisure and then use the toggles to order your tea. I'll be nearby if you need anything."

Both men turned their attention to the rectangle of toggles in the center of the table as she left. The large toggles read *Tea, Sandwiches, Breads, Scones, Sweets,* and *Miscellaneous.* Smaller toggles under each heading allowed patrons to specify certain teas, flavors, types, and so on.

Wallace's eyes were drawn to the last toggle under *Miscellaneous,* which was Wash.

"Let's see what this one does," Thompson said, flipping the toggle.

Both men sat back to wait, and a minute later a door on the far wall swung open. A black iron Scottie dog pulling a little cart behind him trotted to their table and sat back on his haunches, one paw raised to "shake." Wallace chuckled and shook his paw while Thompson spotted the washbasin, towel, and soap.

"I like this Mr. Sharpe," he said, removing his gloves to wash his hands.

The Scottie dog whined and hissed as steam emitted from his ears and trotted off again.

"That was utterly charming! No wonder this place is so popular," Wallace stated, looking about.

Every table was filled with patrons, and the bright striped, yellow wallpaper and the wide, sunny windows allowed everything to be seen clearly. Miniature dirigibles steamed overhead, carrying trays of sweets and sandwiches to tables while the Scottie dog made other appearances, pulling his cart holding steaming teapots and tea services. Little clockwork birds perched in the corners of the room chirped popular melodies, and the red-haired hostess walked through the whole room, making sure that everything was working smoothly.

Thompson and Wallace ordered their tea and watched with delight as the Scottie dog returned to their table, "dancing" on his hind legs as he approached, and dirigibles shaped like mob caps floated down to their table, bearing chicken and ham sandwiches with mustard and watercress, scones with clotted cream, miniature cherry pies, chocolate-covered biscuits, and colorful petit-fours.

"Did you have lunch?" Thompson asked as he stared at the plenitude.

"What do you think?" Wallace returned, feeling his mouth water.

"Good. I didn't, either," Thompson said, placing a napkin on his lap. "Thank God the old man's paying for this. Let's tuck in!"

They made short work of the food and, with two pots of tea to wash it all down, both men leaned back in their chairs, replete. They'd kept their conversation light and desultory whilst they were occupied with their meal; and it was only as they were dabbing at their lips with their napkins, they realized they were the last patrons left.

"Once this is all settled, I'd like to come back." Thompson sighed. "Whoever they have working in the kitchen is a gift from the culinary gods."

"That's very kind of you to say," the red-haired hostess said, taking a seat at the table. She took the last petit-four from the plate, bit into it, and chewed. "Too much salt in this batch. I'll have to check the settings."

"Young woman, are you in the habit of seating yourself at your customers' tables?" Thompson demanded, surprised at her effrontery.

"I am when it's two men with business for me. I'm the proprietor, Lavinia Sharpe, and I know the two of you work for Llewllyn & Company."

She smiled and raised an eyebrow. "A pleasure to meet you."

LOY KRATHONG

BY JEREMY BOCK

Lin peeks out from underneath the stall's awning to look across the field at the Mekong. The river's banks are dry. Only a small stream cuts its way through the mud in the center. The banana trees on the near side stretch their branches wide to soak up the tropical sun. She wipes the sweat from her forehead, exhales, and returns to the shade. This is tradition, but today, it's so damn hot. She should have waited until later in the afternoon to come to the outdoor market. Judging by how few people are here, the other parents thought it better to come later, too. At least she beat the crowd.

"Mommy! I want the yellow one!"

"Ami, calm down. We'll get it," Lin placates her 3-year-old daughter. "The marigold, please," she says in Thai to the older woman behind the piles of flowers on the craft table.

The old auntie sorts through the whites, blues and oranges to find a yellow and clips the flower's stem short. She hands it to Lin who hands it to the toddler. The little girl stabs it right in the center of the pancake-shaped Styrofoam cylinder.

"Oh-oh, you're very good at this!" the old auntie says to Ami. "What would you like next?"

"I want to put banana leaves all around. Like a crown!"

"Good idea!" the auntie says. Lin nods to allow the purchase. The auntie reaches into a basket underneath the table and pulls out a handful of banana leaves pre-cut and folded into neat identical triangles. "Is this your first krathong?" she asks Ami.

"Umm...yes!"

"We floated one last year, but this is her first time making her own," Lin explains.

"It's wonderful you want to keep the tradition," the auntie says.

"My mom took me here when I was little. I moved back from America with my family last year."

"I thought I recognized you." The auntie smiles and looks down to Ami. "Do you know how to put these on?" she asks.

"Umm...no!"

"It can be tricky. You take a toothpick. Be very careful. Don't poke yourself. Very sharp. And you stick it through the side of the leaf here and stick the other end into the foam." The old auntie secures the leaf to the krathong so that the top of the triangle sits above the flat part of the cylinder. "Can you do it?"

Ami picks up a banana leaf and pokes at it uselessly with a toothpick. "Ehhh. Mommy, help!"

Lin exhales through her nose. "Okay." She hunches over the table and starts decorating.

"Mommy, I want a white flower next!"

Lin's husband, Sean, and their eight-year-old son return from their walk around the other stalls. Her boy is licking a popsicle. Her husband has a stick of deep-fried meatballs in one hand and a bottle of beer in the other. Beads of condensation have formed all around the bottle. Lin tilts her head to the side and squints.

"Already?" she asks.

"Hey. It's Sunday."

She straightens up, removes the beer from Sean's hand and takes a sip. It's cold and good.

"Daddy, look!" Ami snatches the half-finished krathong from the table and holds it up to her father's waist. "Is it pretty?"

"Beautiful, baby girl."

"Hey! No fair!" Ami spots her brother's popsicle. "I want one, too!"

"I knew you would." Sean takes a second popsicle out of his pocket and takes off the wrapper before handing it to his daughter. Lin takes the krathong from Ami so she can go for the sugar.

"It's red!" Ami puts the end of the popsicle in her mouth. "And cold."

"Anything for me?" Lin asks.

Her husband gestures with his empty hand. "You said you didn't want anything!"

"I changed my mind." She takes another drink of his beer. "I'm keeping this."

The auntie behind the table motions to Lin to hand her the krathong. "I can finish it for you, dear."

"No. Thank you," Lin says. "We'll finish it."

"Do these things really work, Mom?" her son asks.

Lin smiles and puts her hand on the back of her boy's head, lacing her fingers through his curls wet with sweat. "They're for the water spirits. If we show them respect by floating the krathong, they might give us a big rainstorm and refill the river."

"The only way the krathongs are going to work is if we strap bombs to 'em, go up to China and float 'em at that God-forsaken dam," Sean says. Lin raises her eyebrows at her husband and then looks away.

"Can we?!" her son asks.

"No. But we can put a sparkler on top," Lin says to her boy.

"Yeah, yeah!" Ami shouts and bounces sending popsicle droplets in different directions. Several land on the white parts of her dress.

Lin hands her son twenty baht. "Take Ami and go pick one out." She points to the next vendor over. The boy takes the money and his sister's hand. Lin rests her head on her husband's shoulder and watches their children. He reclaims his beer.

She looks back at the depleted Mekong. "Are we going to be okay?"

"Always." Sean takes a drink "You should finish the krathong, though. Just in case."

Lin lets out a small laugh through her nose and picks up another toothpick and banana leaf.

"That's why we're here."

THE FATHER, THE SON, THE GHOSTS

BY STAN PISLE

He sings every song.
Albums I'll never play again.
I text my brother, "Music is that rift we travel on."
He responds, "Too much riding with the bare Willie?"

It took five downloads from iTunes to cross Pennsylvania.
Storytellers by Johnny Cash and Willie got us from Phillipsburg to Beth-
lehem.
"The Red Headed Stranger" to Harrisburg.
"Unearthed" to the border of West Virginia.

"Jersey Girl" was rejected on the banks of the Delaware.
Billy Joel, an exit outside of Allentown.
I sneak in," Peter Frampton Unplugged."
I'm messing with him.
I'm 54 and still can't play my music.

30 years after escaping the country zoo,
I'm caged again,
in an exhuming story of wanting out.
Of the car, of his mythical Montana ranch,
of being lacquered back into rural childhood.

We visit graveyards of ancestors and friends.
Over parents, aunts, older generations, he utters the same: "Rest in Peace."
A five second ceremony, I bury with a shovel of questions.
They are ignored and it's a country concert again.

At the flight 93 memorial, we stop by Mark Bingham's name.
He asks how I knew him?
Like flushing a covey of quail, I pop off shots:
"He went to Cal, I know his mother, I gave money to this place."
Truths that drop into the souls in the soil beneath.

We're each hunting, with a long-playing record.
A groove that guides us through trees listening for cracks and popples,
that might hide game.
A rut of regret we've been in since my birth.
Dug by his boyhood poverty, I hear the frequent tune.
A guttural ditty repeated anytime I stray from macho.

Why do we both play country?
He's a Montana cowboy with a ranch.
A hunter. His closet full of jackets sewn from the hooved he's slain.
Raised on the banks of the Delaware, he's no more a cowboy than I am
a western author.
But the antelope, salmon, and sparrows fly from my poems.
Notes I play to evoke the emotions from childhood mind tugs.
I write from Berkeley streets, of predators, prey, and bait.
Of squawking conversations between crows and jays,
elks bugling from fog, balanced on tule blades,
and of the fried snake claimed to "taste like chicken" when I was nine.

Somewhere between Uniontown and Morgantown
I realize, country is a handy cover.
Readers can sit across the table from my mystery and not be served
leftovers.
A recipe my off-tune rider spent a whole life fitting me for.
I download another album.

FRAGMENTS: THE LANGUAGE OF DREAMS

By Cerid Jones

Four daddy-long-legs traversed the fine line of an invisible web that ran behind a walnut writing desk. A misleading object, bought by a man who never wrote a word at it.

He liked the idea of it; so, as he was accustomed to often do, he pushed the wad of cash across the counter. 'Experts' were called in to take it apart, just to fit the cumbersome thing through the narrow bedroom door.

Until recently, it sat depressed and empty, abandoned. Constantly referred to as *his*. When she moved into the room, a room which once smelled of un-smoked Drumm- a scent she couldn't name till she was 18 - and now reeked of charred Riverstone; she cluttered the discarded desk with obscure, agitated, and predominately useless things for a desk such as this to contain. It wasn't *her* desk, and the tainted feel of its pre-imposed image stained her treatment of it with distain.

Thus, when Nio moved into the room, she was content to allow its spiders to claim the gaping wooden structure as a frame to anchor their dust collectors from.

One had caught a moth.

The others clearly hungry.

Without violence or aggression, they advanced, one tentative step at a time, from behind the desk.

The she-spider, abdomen fat with carriage, deterred them with a flick of a spindled arm – or perhaps leg,

is there a difference with spiders?

Back and forth this retreat and advance played out, rhythmical and tense. Nio plagued with sleepless nights, lounging in her bed, watching, entranced, till Morpheus called her in.

Concrete bridges protrude between parking-lots
and alley ways,

motorways....

and brothels.
Graffiti marking memories, monuments to moments of a time and place
unspoken....

yet devoted
to a permanent impermanence in the underbelly of the city
where the living lend themselves to truths
walking suits

abuse.....

Nio watched her morning coffee breathe against her windscreen. The car was still. Dormant, incapable of use. Not because *it* was lacking but because *she* was.

An American Woman's evolution hummed out from the stereo, ballads bellowing out things Nio kept well below the surface. If she couldn't speak, sometimes another 'she' could sing or say it for her. It seemed to relieve the pressure that pushed against her temples, gnawed under her skin, keeping her molars clenched.

The tempest of her mind was not easily stilled. Alone, in her dormant car Nio could attempt to let it wash over her and, perhaps, seep out.

The window wound down; a cigarette hung between worn green fingernails. Limp in the deflation of the morning air. Each puff hungry for serenity.

A fly saw the opening; evaded the hand, bypassed the smoke, and invaded inside.

It traced the circumference of the wheel purposefully, like it knew its secrets.

She watched it, jealous of its ability.

————◆————

In the city of the blind
who see more than one might think,
the one eyed wonder
is not king
but observer,
is not wise from sight but
blind....
from vision.....

————◆————

Rain rattled the leaves of the adjacent trees. Its light mist like a virgin's kiss upon the soil. It had been dry for months now.

The lovers who birthed the world, the god of sky, Ranginui, and goddess of earth, Papatūānuku, were alive again. Under the veranda Nio was transfixed as Rangi's tears laced, Papa's skin, the relief in it palatable. Rangi's long absence had left Papa quaking for the tender offerings of her distant mate. Papa does not move for the mighty Rā as he beats his relentless fiery gaze down upon her in the dry hot days of summer.

Don't underestimate the female soul when it is left in yearning, she can and will shift your foundations.

Water wept itself into welts upon the earth, so dry it could not drink its depth, it overflowed, flooded. The witness of the reunion, a needed destruction in the unity of coupling, sent shivers through her.

Even the air held the scent of lovers; to some a stench, but to her, it was sweetness. If she could, she would wrap herself in this delicacy and succumb to its succulent delights. But it was far too dangerous to try to play with gods.

⸺◈⸺

In these alleyways'
woman are wanton of men to make them full of belly and bare of body.
They are not harlots,
not harpies,
not harpers or
whores;
they are half whole and holy in their holes.
Their smiles speak of scars and sacred screams,
stories seldom spoken,
but when they are,
are soft and sweet and sorrowful,
sobering and savoury.

⸺◈⸺

Crickets cried in the depth of the night. An eerie stillness suspended itself on the air. Nio smoked.

Shadows slinked across the silvery face; silhouettes splattered sporadically in the distance. It was a blood moon, so they said.

She watched. Waited. Let herself, mind and body, be still.

Drenched, the harvest faced moon was soaked in a mulled fire and the world became silent, thick, almost touchable, nearly malleable.

She thought about ancient times; the red-haired maidens lined up to be bled out so the demons wouldn't eat the moon, so the sun would rise. Her daddy told her about that when she was 8 and she watched the sun be eaten for the first time.

When she was 12, she started dyeing her hair red.

⸺◈⸺

There is no hiding here.
This city's streets are sacrament,
streaked with spit and blood and cum.
Honesty hosting histories; nothing is swept away.
From the debris of decay fauna flourishes from the fragments,
from the sapropel springs salicaceous shrines,
salsify shoots,
sinister Stereaceae,
sacred Solanaceae,
and the salvifical southernwood.
Rotting roadkill rises anew in
fly agaric formations, the salutations of cyclic transformations.
This city is not afraid to be bare boned and blood brave and weeping.

------◆------

Red berries, vibrant against the green foliage seemed to speak of a silent violence, whispering something pernicious beneath the surface. Black birds pecked at them, cocking their heads with inquisitive looks.

Nio watched. Enamoured by their beauty, but simultaneously disturbed by the black, green, red and white display, as if an alluring violation.

She could hear hollow words spilling out of her mouth while he proclaimed, for the hundredth time as he ran shaking hands through black hair, how much she had torn his world apart. How much he loved her, how he could see his life with her... She should feel guilty that she didn't care. Was that such a horrible thing?

Things end, love can be parasitic, it's not always eternal.

At first, she was proud to be the prize, but over time, the presumption of her dumbness developed into a cancer. The lies threaded into layers, so thick that Nio was buried beneath them. Now, only a comfortable numbness remained.

It irritated her that relationships had to be so complicated, so fragile. Her lips moved, but she could no longer hear what words she was saying. Nio kept her eyes fixed out the window.

Another bird landed, tore the white flesh from the red skin as it snatched its prey from the victim, all the while its beady black eyes stared coldly into hers.

━━━◆○◆━━━

The pilgrimage is persistent and holds a purpose in the pointless precision
of promise,
the souls here are priests of primal patronage, honest and raw.
Peace found in upholding the acceptance of the individual,
knowing that all here are seekers of the same serenity within their sins,
for all is sin
and there is no god to garnish it.
There is no shame,
no shade of secrecy.
Here, in this city
your true self is thrust from your depth you are forced to face your frame
unfortified by false
furnishings.
If you find fear in it,
if it feasts and ferments and you find yourself at your fingent, facinorous,
One of two factions will be your fate:
you will find yourself in such disdain that you can choose naught but to
tear yourself from limb to limb and pray your particles find way
to begin again,
or
you will turn and flee to some other fairground and play out your days
in the world's best laid out charade.

━━━◆○◆━━━

Pulling her hood down over her face, Nio adjusted her sepia tinted glasses as she was coached through the foreign city. Her eyes wide and hungry as she tried to lap up every detail.

Searching for substance under the servitude of the action.

The remnants of the past lingered in archaic structures, collaged between convex coated glass, reaching skyward, turning reflections into cubist masterpieces. Yellows, oranges, reds, and youthful greens lined the faceless grey of the concrete; the old oak trees in autumn were painting life back into the streets. There was irony there. It was beautiful, that was true, but it was the same as the make-up on the young girls who flicked their hair and batter worn eyelids. Behind the image lay a vast emptiness, it left her feeling sick.

———◆○◆———

Here my friend, is truth
and you will find it marked on the map;
here be dragons. ...
In this city there lurks many lackaday lamisters,
but not all are dragged behind black eyed daemons,
there are those obambulate beings
who open admittance to optical obsessions
and in themselves become
illuminated.
These beings balance and baisemain one another.
Their need forms a nexus, navigating and narrating their ontal Oneiro-
mancy.

———◆○◆———

Barefooted and brave Nio walks through the supermarket, met by the masquerade of hollow souls in daily living. Waves of judgement solidify. It becomes difficult to put one foot in front of the other, like every step must break the web these tarantulas have shat out at her.

They fear to meet her eyes. Bodies pulse with rejections, as if to force her as far away from themselves as they can. Their eyes feed upon her, as if they could use their expression of disdain to suck out authenticity like blood from a straw.It's crippling.

She wonders how long it's been since they feed as the weight of their contrition burrows into her. Nio senses how hollow they are, already bled dry by the performance they long to sustain, judgements before being judged, status acquired by possession, obsessed with finding place in the empty cavern of conformity. She wonders if they fed on one another like this, survival forcing them to assimilate.

She thinks of the spiders in her room and isn't sure which role she is in now; the moth, the feeder, or the hungry.

⸻◆⸻

Saluki's sulk in the shadows of the sidewalk,
salivating at the sight of samite silked Soldiers swallowing salep,
saliferous sweat seeping from their sorrows.
Selfishly seeking silence,
they slink into shady spirit spilled shacks.
Faded caffoy lamp shades hang askew from a carpet coated celling,
beaded curtains bounce in the breeze from the barkeeps window.
Inside, smoke stretches the air into a caliginous coat of cobwebs.
Those here do not need to see to move where they desire.
The barkeep knows his patrons by footstep
has their poison poured long before they
position themselves on their perverse pedestals.
The soldiers sip by the serenade of shotguns
salute to samogon hits as if it would be a sanatorium
for suffering.
The other ebrious entities enchant themselves in endlessly
egelidating empty glasses,
their eyes ebb from focus to fictions and their mouths macarize in macrol-
ogy
while their words whisper
wanzed wishes.
They pass out into pacificated states of
papaverous pandemonium,
peaceful in pleasant slumbers....

⸻◆⸻

As she slipped out from the borrowed bed, the butt of her cigarette dropped in the empty bottle on the nightstand, smoke still blew through her nose.

Taking a slash, Nio caught her nakedness in the mirror as she washed her hands; white flesh, near on glowing in the dim light of the hotel room. Ghostly.

He was still in bed, bright eyed, green, full of hope and wonderment.

He smiled at her, sighing sweetly. Adoration drenched.

The bile built in her throat.

He was saying something about happiness and love and wonder and bliss and oneness. Nio wore her painted smile. She hadn't meant to, she never meant to.

Like a stray dog, she'd brought him to shelter, hope-fed him, bathed him, loved him, stripped away his inhibitions, uncaged him. Now... she was about to put her jeans on and walk out the door, leaving him in open skies he didn't know how to navigate, vulnerable and alone. She hadn't meant to.

Nio, simply, wished to show him the beautiful creature he was, how he could glow and grow in a world of grey.

Breaking cages can break people, she still doesn't understand how, doesn't know why.

Outside the hotel room, she throws up in the gutter.

⎯⎯◆◇◆⎯⎯

Upstairs,
prostitutes pretend to pant and are paid to be
penetrated by the partially flaccid penises of the
pissed peddlers.
Under their fake fuck me faces they laugh at the simplicity of their sport.
These women are not lacking in self-respect,
they are not dirty
or demoralized,
they are the empowered empresses of ecstasy.
The men here know their power
and facundly fear it.

*The nympholepsy leaves them to a nectariferous narcotic
negligence and thus
Morpheus mews sweetly in their slumber.*

A moth flew in the open window, traced itself across her fingers, and flew out again.

A daddy-long-legs lost its footing and fell down behind the dresser.

Nio feels her stomach drop, cave in; she'd be bleeding by morning. She supposes, that is a good thing.

Head hurting, pulled into the fragments of the billions of existences she can't entirely understand. Burying her face into the nook of her elbow, she ignores the damp heat that leaks out the corners of her eyes...

She slept, glad to dream, it gave her a world that made sense, but the older Nio gets, the less sure she is of which she dreams, and which she walks.

WILD LIFE

LOST ISLE OF BUZIOS

BY GEORGE LIES

Bogart Sicani swam with ease through the ocean waves which rolled behind him onto the gray sand of the Isle of Buzios—his destination one hundred meters in front of him. Like Ulysses long ago, he stroked towards the Great Rocks, which had been thrown to earth by the hand of the Giant Cyclops during the time of the gods. Seagulls screeched overhead; the shear of one wave overlapped another, washing over him. He tried shouting his joy but could not; so he sucked air and ducked beneath the surface.

In the depths, he felt the muffled silence. He swam past a school of silver fish, a spiny creature, a slithering eel; and the clams nestled in the silky strands of onion flora for his family's soup, the hide-and-seek of squids, which tasted like salty pineapple after roasting. He bobbed to the surface and gasped as a wave rolled over him. He could not yell his name although he desired to hear the name of Bogart Sicani echo off the Great Rocks.

The gods had betrayed him at his birth. They had not given him a voice.

He swam on until he reached the white sand of the inlet, the rhythm of waves stroking the beach, shrouded by large black rocks. For his own fun, he crawled like a crab the last few meters onto land. He snarled in silence as he reached the beach. He collapsed on his back and looked skyward. He tried screaming to the gods, but he knew they could hear nothing.

Bogart felt air enter his chest, his lungs rise and fall, taking in the oxygen. He heard the blanket of ocean water cloak the beach. But no sound could he make. He lay there flapping his arms like a seagull in the sand, creating a swath of angel wings on both sides. The clouds passed, playing hide-and-seek with the sun; he opened his eyes, wanting to scream his hate for the gods. He squinted and felt warmth from words he imagined, those of his grandmother's: "one day the gods will give you a voice."

She had crafted him a musical instrument at age six, a whistling tonette and he had practiced blowing into its thin lips, his fingers fluttering over air holes, summoning flute-like tunes that made his grandmother sway. He played it as the pair journeyed across the Isle of Buzios, as they hiked woodsy trails below the Great Volcano; she'd gesture, telling how the mountain once breathed red fire and dust. While he clung to her sheepskin, she told stories of gods above and sea monsters in the ocean. Here, she pointed at a snow-capped dark mountain, where Zeus tossed the Titans into the Great Volcano when they betrayed him. Pointing there, she showed him where she found lava-burned wood for crafting his gift of sound.

Lying on the sand, he opened his eyes as clouds eclipsed the sun. He scrambled to his feet and turned toward the Great Rocks. He wondered how a one-eyed Giant could throw boulders so far from his mountain cave and, even more, how he detected Ulysses' ships in the sea although being blinded by the swift thrust of a spear. The Great Rocks stretched around the ocean inlet like a black collarbone he once found from a butchered ox. He counted one, two, three, four peaks. That cyclops had thrown four missiles into the sky, on that day long ago, and without eyesight, trying to wreck Ulysses' escape back home.

Now Bogart began climbing the face of the Black Rocks, heading to the summit. Hand over heel, he navigated slippery ledges, crevices and footholds. With the wind rustling his hair, he stood at the top; he took in the view of forest and land that stretched to the Sea of Atlantis. His grandmother had told him of distant voyagers that shared the water route and how the treacherous waters had kept invader tribes far from the Isle of Buzios. On her last day, she whispered in Bogart's ear and said, play your sound; the gods will listen, even the sea monsters will heed your voice.

Bogart readied himself now for playing music to the gods. From his satchel, treated with waxen olive oil to protect against salt water, he pulled out his tonette and sat on a flat stone slab. Around him the ocean turbulence roused the seascape's horizon. Beyond the rocks, as his grandmother had described, sea monsters stirred the waters. Gargantuan Scylla often grew agitated in her cave and, across the strait, the serpentine Charybdis created whirlpools. He wondered how his own islanders' fishing trawlers ever survived their wrath.

Bogart undid the wrapping which held the instrument dry. His fingers filled the seven holes of the surface, his thumb fit the underside hole. He cleared his lungs and began creating music like he had for his grandmother before she left his world. He took a breath and pushed air into the tonette as his fingertips danced in sequence.

The sound rose from the Rocks, and the sea turned calm, the serpents listening. The soft tone caressed the ocean, smoothed the rough waves to a standstill, and swept far away, toward the horizon where Atlas stood at the edge of the world. He paused for air before striking a high chilling note that made the sound reverse and return. The sound echoed off the Great Rocks and spiraled like a helix skyward, toward the realm of the gods. Bogart paused, thinking the gods must hear his plea.

The gods heard. The boy's sounds pleased them. It was time to give him a voice and Zeus finally gave the order.

Bogart turned away from the Sea of Atlantis. From his perspective atop the Black Rocks, he tried screaming his name, but no sound came out. Having faith in his grandmother's foresight, he blew into the tonette and yelled his name again.

Out came a new sound that he heard: Bogart Sicani.

He heard. He heard his name bounce off the Black Rocks and roll down the cliffs and across the black sands; the first words his vocal cords ever made. Sounds mixed with the hissing of seagulls overhead and the rush of waves caressing the shore.

He looked across the vast waters, back toward his homeland.

He could not believe now what he saw. A firestorm spurted from the Great Volcano, and red smoke spurted out, a red burning lava flowing like a river all the way to the sea, a flow of bright red coming down the mountain and blanketing thick forests like a flood moving across the land. Seawater rose around the Isle of Buzios; the land began submerging beneath the ocean's surface.

Now he feared for his people.

Bogart weighed his next action. He held the tonette to his lips and played musical sounds again. He stopped and yelled his name three times more. Sounds floated across the waters to his Isle of Buzios; his people listened and shouted praise. They began running toward the music, to the shore's edge and to their boats. Their vessels' sails unfurled as they set forth on a new journey. Like Ulysses, they began their escape across the sea.

PHYSICAL FITNESS AND THE CHIPMUNK FACTOR

By Janis-Rozena Peri

"Cynthia, unless you want to develop full-fledged diabetes, heart complications, and/or have a stroke, you must lose weight and exercise. This is non-negotiable if you want to live a long healthy life."

Such a pronouncement from my physician finally caught my attention. Thus, I was spurred on to begin an intense physical fitness program which included suggestions chattered by some truly obnoxious chipmunks.

Chipmunks spend much of their time running up and down trees, so they are extremely concerned about physical fitness issues. Human tendencies toward sloth and inactivity fill them with contempt, horror, and righteous indignation. Their expertise was a vital part of my program.

How did I become involved with chipmunks? Actually, we have a relatively uneventful but cordial relationship, a friendly détente, if you will. I stop my car respectfully when the furry little beasts stage some of their innumerable social gatherings in the middle of the street.

The chipmunks, in kind, look away, keeping their snickering to a minimum, when I bike, walk, and/or make other pathetic attempts at physical fitness.

Through the machinations of Rupert, Director-General of the Morgantown Chipmunk Consortium, I was chosen as the main communications liaison of the Human-to-Chipmunk program. My being chosen was somewhat serendipitous.

I was walking through the Arboretum at the very moment local chipmunks were meeting to discuss the need for closer ties with the human community.

Ever practical, Rupert said, "Hey, there's a human walking this way. She'll be so freaked out we can communicate that she'll be unable to speak. We'll appoint her by acclimation."

That's pretty much how it happened.

After a spirited debate among members of the Healthy Human committee, we decided I would train for two athletic events: the Charleston Distance Walk/Run and the Hocking Hills State Park (Ohio) Indian Run. Since this is all new for me, I would walk both events.

Undeterred by some of the chipmunks' worried looks and furious chattering, especially pertaining to the Hocking Hills chipmunk constituency, I began a training routine.

The Charleston Distance Walk/Run was first, giving me an unrealistically pleasant view of this kind of event.

The runners and walkers did parallel but separate races. (The Charleston chipmunks have boycotted the Distance Walk for years. There was some ancient dispute, the nature of which is a mystery. Therefore, the event is chipmunk-free.)

Wonderful, smiling, carefully coiffed women and men were at every corner with water, cookies, encouragement, and directions on where to go next. And last, but far from least, there were carefully placed portable toilets.

Then came Hocking Hills.

First of all, I should have paid more attention to the name of the event: the Hocking HILLS State Park Indian Run. Reputation notwithstanding, Ohio is not a great piece of flat land. It has extremely varied terrain, and it had not occurred to me I would be walking uphill most of the race.

When I arrived at the site, I noticed officials were placing highway cones along the roads in and out of the park. I gladly assumed this meant I would be walking on paved roads. Not.

When I checked in, I was told to get on the next bus to the starting line, which was deep in the woods. Taking one look at the racecourse, I quickly wimped out of the 10K and went for the 5K. There were blue ribbons tied to trees for 5K walkers and runners, and orange ribbons for 10K walkers and runners.

I followed these ribbons as best I could while (1) walking through a forest, not one inch of which was level; (2) avoiding being flattened by runners; (3) figuring out how to keep a steady walking pace over muddy, slippery ground covered with wet leaves and gullies; (4) walking along parts of the path which followed an unknown body of water which was among Ohio's 8,000,000 creeks, ponds, streams, puddles, and or ditches; (5) trying to figure out which way to go when orange and blue ribbons converged, then suddenly disappeared; (6) trying not to be intimidated by park chipmunks, most of whom were laughing at me hysterically [there are rude chipmunks at Hocking Hills State Park]; and (7) ignoring hardy-looking people who sailed by me saying things like, "Only two-and-a-half more miles to go" and "Isn't this fun?"

When I got to the point, I thought was the end, in truth, I had another mile to go, uphill, on a paved road. I had to dodge runners and automobiles. As I dragged myself along with my last breath, about a half mile from the finish line, an absolutely beautiful woman, in glamorous slacks and sandals, walked leisurely by me, not at all winded. She explained she wasn't actually doing the race. She just came out to meet her husband who was running the 60K. No mistake. 60K.

I finally reached the finish line. Aside from the fact that every single muscle in my body was either in pain or in spasm, I had a wonderful time. In the future, irritating as those little animals may be, I shall seek out more chipmunk input in my physical fitness plans.

Perhaps in the future, I'm going to investigate the possibility of a mixed species gym.

A Taste of Huntin Season

By Stan Pisle

Meat comes pre-Spiced in the sagebrush.
Fawns lose spots on spring shoots.
Quail, and chucker fledge on sage seeds.
With assassination, pluckin, and fryin,
your dad utters: "Tastes 'JUST' like chicken."
Not chicken from your childhood, a chicken from his.
A time when meat was smoked by sage branches,
never fresh,
probably rotten,
chickens ran wild back then.
Corn and barley were luxuries not to be afforded to a chicken.
They, apparently, ate sagebrush.

The next meal will be: shot duck or deer.
It'll taste like sage too.

Your Dad will be too chicken to admit why he shot it.
Too chicken to admit why he owns a gun.
Too chicken to say why he thinks sage tastes like chicken.

Then you'll be out huntin.
After a football game, in the car with Chloe,
you'll finally get your sights on her lips, her eyes,

and when your tongue fires,
she tastes like sage too.

But you'll be too chicken to admit that,
and you'll tell a huntin story instead.

NONE SO BLIND—THE ADVENT

By Alan O'Conner

The secret to our silent movement is the moccasins. That and walking on the leaves and not through them. This remote part of the reservation is sacred, so we're more reverent than usual. We weave through giant white oaks, sugar maples and honey locust trees to reach the secret place.

Three of his strides ahead of me is my father, Akatena Wehali, Keen Sighted Eagle. He's a Cherokee Chieftain, CEO of the Bear Paw Resort and Casino, the business that puts food on our table and pays the reservation's bills.

I live in two universes, native heir to Tsalagi Tribe leadership and ordinary student attending Appalachian Regional High School. Dad says that learning the ways of the native and the non-native makes a better man. So, I suck it up and humor his rituals, although I'm more comfortable carrying a cell phone than this antique spear.

This Monomakhus thing has me worried. Like, I might fail or worse. This rite of passage thing, going from boyhood to manhood is mandatory for all Cherokee kids. Monomakhus means the one who hunts alone. So tonight, I must stay in the forest, alone and blindfolded. Non-natives are kids into adulthood, my dad says. The white man has no similar crossing over, like I care.

I stumble over a fallen tree limb, stagger to my feet, then tumble into my father, barely missing him with this stupid spear. He is unmoved, like

I had hit the elm tree beside him. He pushes my shoulders back, adjusts the hawk feather in my leather headband, and looks me square in the eye.

"You are too eager, Red Fox, too nervous," his arm goes around my shoulder. I lean in. "You can do this," he says.

"Is this the place for my execution, I mean my Monomakhus?"

"That's good. Keep with the jokes. They will help you relax. Not here, but there." He points to a small meadow below an opening in the canopy. The scent of alfalfa and clover says we're approaching from downwind. He stops abruptly and I almost bump into him again. "Get down," he whispers, and we crouch behind some junipers.

I see it too. A large black bear feeding on raspberries in the meadow.

"Gunage Yona, a black bear, she's upwind. We smell her, but she hasn't smelled us yet."

From over his shoulder, he removes the ceremonial medicine bag he brought for my Monomakhus. He pulls out a buffalo horn and uncovers the mouth. Inside is a red goop that he quietly administers on himself like war paint. First under his eyes, then the ear lobes, tip of the nose, eyelids, forehead and temples. He dabs a spot on his heart, then lips, followed with a touch of the tongue. His face recoils like he licked a lemon.

"What is this stuff?"

"The Elixir of Eternal Spiritual Connection."

"The what?"

"It was for your Monomakhus, but now I need it."

"What for?

"To connect to the bear." He slips away without further explanation. I shrug.

In the meadow Gunage Yona, the black bear, stops eating. She lifts her nose into the wind, and her massive, furry body rises to a standing position. The meadow is egg-shaped, and I imagine it to be the face of a clock. Her location, twelve o'clock. I stay downwind at the four o'clock spot. Her nose points to ten o'clock, upwind.

Through the sassafras comes Dad. He avoids eye contact with the bear. He hops on a large fallen tree, instantly, he's three feet taller. When added to the extra foot his headdress gives him, and you put it all on top of his six-foot-three-inch frame, he's made himself look big. Now he makes eye contact, and speaks to her softly with a reassuring tone, words coming slowly at first, then moderately.

The bear appears calm as if hypnotized. The bear snorts back, like a pig. Slowly at first and then faster, louder, mirroring Dad's initial cadence. She snaps her jaw several times making a popping sound, and then she roars, but only once.

He breaks eye contact, backs away along the log, adding five feet to the gap. I focus on my breathing so as not to pee my pants.

The bear swats the ground, first with her right paw, then the left. Bear and man freeze facing each other like gunfighters. The forest goes silent. All living things must be as fixated as me. Then the impossible happens. The bear turns, snorts like she's saying goodbye and exits at the two o'clock position.

I rush to my dad's side keeping both eyes on the two o'clock position. "Whoa Dude, oops, I mean whoa Dad! You rock!" I throw my arms around him, and we fall off the log. He pulls me to him, and we wrestle, both of us laughing like when I was a kid.

"You mean we rock, the bear and me."

"You're amazing. You owned her."

"No, son. Bear and I connected, thanks to the elixir. Can you believe that?"

"I believe that you believe it."

"But you saw us. We spoke as single parents. She is bulking up to hibernate and birth twins, and me guiding you doing the Monomakhus. We were connected."

"Connected to a bear, really? You need to check what's in that stuff." I snicker.

"Didn't you see us talking?"

"I saw you scope the meadow, enter upwind, respect her escape routes, avoid her berries, give her space and show no fear. Textbook, Bear 101."

"You missed our connection."

"Telling you what I saw. Have I failed the Monomakhus?"

"No, but it'll be harder. Alone and blindfolded, the elixir and your spear are your only weapons against that which would harm you. Do you still want to do this?"

"I promised I would. You say the goop is part of our deal, then I'm down with that."

"Here son, let me help you get this on."

THE TALES OF SIR BISCUIT

By Lore Lee

I sat, perched on Chatinept's chest, staring at her eyelids, anticipating their opening, waiting for her to respond to my presence... I continued waiting... and waiting.

"Hey," I said. She failed to react. "Hey," I said louder. Still nothing.

With grace, with majestic restraint, I reached out and brushed her nose. Once, twice, a third time. Her hand rose up to swat away the touch, but otherwise, she didn't stir.

"Good morning," I sang. And when there was no response, I took aim and batted her chin. "HEY!" Chatinept opened her eyes and let out a series of grunts and groans. "Good morning," I sang again.

We descended the stairs, and I wove myself between her lumbrous limbs, leading the way and showing my appreciation for her attention and forthcoming presentation of my first meal of the day. She let out a series of indecipherable squawks, suggesting frustration for something that only Chatinept could comprehend. Her foot brushed against me with wanton disregard for my safety and her sounds of irritation turned to penitence.

"I forgive you," I offered. I continued down the steps and into the hallway, doubling back to ensure she was following. "I forgive you, but let's stay on task."

In an instant, I sensed something was wrong, truly wrong, gravely wrong. My nose twitched as a fetid scent drifted into the hallway from the kitchen.

Danger!

I puffed up my coat and twitched my tail. "Stop, stop, stop," I chattered to Chatinept, keeping my eyes on the end of the hall. "There's something in the kitchen. Don't go in there!"

She ignored my warning and walked past me. I chattered again, but chased after her, fearful some calamity would befall my ward. Like a child, crawling toward a vacuum cleaner, blissfully ignorant of their own mortality, Chatinept trundled into the kitchen.

I froze at the threshold, staring at the spoiled thing before me. Its face was misshapen and stained with rot. It moved with slow twists and jerks, each limb ending in a swarming mass of fleshy twigs. Chatinept ignored the aberration's presence and instead moved to the fridge, closer to it.

I leaped onto the counter to pull her attention away from her task, to make her realize her life was in danger from the thing now towering over her.

"Hawp," Chatinept called out. She hurried over to me, clapping her hands together in quick succession. She uttered nonsense words meant to harass me until I jumped to the floor.

Though she didn't understand what I was saying, she was at least out of the horror's reach. It turned toward me and bared its teeth, broken and stained, and I hissed in reply. If it was a battle of wills the shade wanted, it would find me a worthy adversary; I could wait an eternity.

I hissed at it again and Chatinept recoiled from me instinctually, thinking it was intended for her. She said something in surprise and laughed at me. Such blissful, childish ignorance.

Having the cryptid's attention, I ran with full speed out of the kitchen and into the dining room, hoping to draw it away from my clumsy pridemate. I stopped, turned, stared in wild-eyed expectancy. It hadn't taken the bait. I barreled back into the kitchen, lest Chatinept move nearer its grasp.

Chatinept laughed again and shook her head. Oblivious, she walked to the countertop and began to open a can of food for me.

"Thank you," I said. Now wasn't the time, but I found it difficult to contain my enthusiasm. It smelled divine. "Thank you," I said again.

"Meow?" Chatinept asked.

"Thank you," I said again, more slowly, hoping she would understand.

"Meow?"

I looked at her with frustration and turned my attention back to the long-limbed creature slowly making its way across the kitchen. Its body was covered in a cracked and infected carapace, and small hairs sprouted here and there. It reeked of anger and malevolence. I scooted under the table and chairs in the middle of the kitchen and batted at its feet.

Growling, it leaned down to seize me, those milky eyes fixed on mine. I dodged between the chairs, using them like armor. My small size and agility outmatched its strength and enormity. I swatted at its fingers and wove between the table legs.

Chatinept asked me a question as she began mixing dry kibble into the meaty puree from the can.

Now that I had the terror's regard, I bolted for the dining room once again. It followed, vaulting over the table with more dexterity than I gave it credit for. A fleeting sense of panic coursed through my body; I shook it out as the thing grew closer.

It picked me up into its massive grip, squeezing my ribs tighter and tighter. "Ch- He-" I tried to call out to Chatinept, but no words came.

I bared my teeth and bit into its wrist. Its blood was thick and yellow. The taste of death and decay oozed onto my tongue. I landed on my feet as it released me, and I caught my breath.

I sprang to the curio cabinet and then at its neck, knocking a lamp onto the floor in the process. I charged with my claws presented and sunk my bite into its jugular as I heard Chatinept yell something from the kitchen. She had heard the commotion.

Bringing the beast down, I tore a final chunk from its throat and spat it onto the carpeted floor. Chatinept appeared in the hallway, hands on her hips. She looked less than pleased.

"You're welcome," I said.

I walked past her, leaving my fallen foe behind me. I yearned for breakfast and, as I entered the kitchen once again, I saw my oblivious companion had finished preparing it. I looked up and Chatinept was still there, hands on hips.

"Thank you," I said.

KIN

By Edwina Pendarivis

"The ivory-billed woodpecker was last sighted in 1924, in Osceola County, Florida." Nine-year-old Larry laid the W-X-Y-Z volume of the encyclopedia aside, closed his eyes, and subtracted 1924 from 1950. Twenty-six years! He'd never get to see one of those birds. He read on, "Native Americans prized woodpeckers as symbols of courage. Because these birds could make a great hole in a tree, their feathers might lend that power to a warrior who needed to make a great hole in the enemy."

Thunder rumbled.

Pushing Ghost, the family's big tom cat, off his lap, he got up and hurried to the door. All along the street, palm leaves thrashed in the wind. Dark clouds scudded across the sky over Tampa. Larry laughed in excitement and stepped onto the porch. He grabbed the handlebars of his bike and rolled it down the steps. The first raindrops plopped onto his bare shoulders. Then the torrent started.

"Wait!" Sylvia called, tugging her tricycle toward the steps, "Wait for me!"

He took off as soon as his sister got to the sidewalk. Sylvia hunched forward, pedaling fast. Wings of water rose from the tires of passing cars, splattering the children and adding to their fun. A couple of blocks later, they rode onto the playground.

Sylvia climbed on the merry-go-round. "Push me."

"You'll get dizzy and throw up," her brother said.

"I won't. I promise."

"Go on the slicky-slide."

She sat there stubbornly. Larry gave the hexagonal bench a shove to get it going and walked to the swing set. Grabbing the cross bar, he practiced skinning-the-cat until he was dizzy.

"Swing me, Larry," Sylvia said, running up to him,

The two played until the storm passed and the asphalt got too hot for their bare feet.

"Let's go home," Larry said. Sweaty and tired, Sylvia didn't protest.

As soon as they walked in the door, their grandmother ordered, "Get those wet clothes off!" Pointing her cane at them, she asked "Where'd you go?"

"Playground," Sylvia called over her shoulder as she hurried to the bathroom to peel off her sunsuit. Wrapping a towel around herself, she pattered into the bedroom she and her mother shared to get dressed. Larry went into his and granny's bedroom to pull his wet shorts off and put a dry pair on.

After they were dressed, Granny patted the couch for Sylvia to sit beside her and said, "Turn on the radio for us."

Larry lay on the floor, propped up on his elbows, to read more about woodpeckers.

"Always got his nose in a book," the old woman harrumphed before turning her attention to The Guiding Light.

"Tune it in," Larry said, frowning at the loud static. Sylvia twisted the dial until the program came in clearly. She sat still a few minutes then went to the kitchen to play with Butterscotch's kittens. She picked one up, cuddled it under her chin, then put it down and picked up the next one until she'd hugged all five. Just as she was putting the last kitten down, a man appeared at the back door. He called to her softly through the screen, "Sylvia, Daddy's home."

Sylvia got to her feet. Without looking toward the door again, she walked out of the kitchen into the living room, where she lay down with her head in her grandmother's lap. Butterscotch was curled up in the corner of the sofa, and Sylvia stretched out one leg to tickle the cat's soft belly with her toes. She looked at the clock over the mantle to see where the hands pointed. Every now and then she glanced at the front door to see if a man was standing there.

Just before the clock's hands made one line, straight up and down, she heard her mother's footsteps on the porch. Larry got up to unlatch the screen door.

"Mama!" Sylvia called, sliding off the couch.

Their mother rode the bus home from work, and both children waited impatiently for six o'clock.

"Are you hungry?" Mildred asked as she headed toward the kitchen, grocery bag in her arms. "How about hamburgers for supper?" Sylvia, Larry, and Granny followed.

"They went outside without asking," Granny tattled.

"You know better than that," Mildred said, frowning in Larry's direction as she put the groceries on the counter. While the ground beef patties fried, she set the table. To brighten the mood, she reached to the top shelf for their best drinking glasses—iridescent goldish-orange and pink-hued carnival glass. As she reached for the glasses, she noticed her hands, the short fingernails suited to her work as a typist, no nail polish, and no ring.

After she'd washed the supper dishes, Mildred wiped the table clean so Larry could work on his transistor radio kit. It was dark outside by the time she finished household chores and got around to feeding the cats. Sylvia was in bed, and Larry was unplugging his soldering iron on his mother's direction to put everything away.

She'd just stepped out to the back steps to empty scraps into the cats' food bowls when she saw a man standing nearby.

"Hello, Mildred."

"Cliff!" she said." My god! Cliff! You scared me! How long have you been out there? What are you . . . good heavens!"

"Aren't you going to invite me in?" he asked with a half-smile, dropping his cigarette and grinding it under the toe of his shoe.

"Well, yes, of course. Come on, come on in," she said, holding the door open for him. His motorcycle—the same one he'd ridden away on four years ago—was parked on the sidewalk between her house and the one next door.

Larry stood up, fury sweeping through the youngster. Without conscious thought, but with sure aim, he hurled the soldering iron. Its hot metal tip hit just below the man's right eye, gouging out a triangle of flesh. "Get out! Get out!"

His mother rushed to him and held him tight to console him and keep him from attacking his father. He twisted wildly, trying to escape her grasp. Anger clouded Cliff's features, but he spoke calmly, looking at Mildred, not at his son.

"Maybe I deserved that." He touched his face and reached for the dish towel to wipe blood away.

Granny toddled into the kitchen to see what the commotion was about. She stopped just inside the doorway, leaning on her cane. She couldn't quite place the man, though he looked like someone she should know.

"Would you like some coffee or iced tea?" she asked him, raising her voice so she could be heard over the sound of Larry's shouts and Mildred's repeated "hush now."

Next morning, at about dawn, Mildred got up from the couch, sweaty from the embrace in which she and Cliff had spent the night. He grabbed her wrist, pulling her back down.

She protested quietly, not wanting to wake her mother or the children. "I've got to get ready for work."

He flung her wrist away, and she left the room, embarrassed at her doughy near nakedness. Cliff laid back. A weight landed on his chest, and he was looking into the baleful yellow eyes of a big tom cat. He grabbed it by the scruff of the neck and tossed it over the coffee table into the middle of the room. Ghost glared at him, hissed, and then prowled away. Cliff rolled over and went back to sleep.

One week later, two adults and two children stood in a yard in rural Osceola County watching the rented car carrying Cliff and Mildred disappear down the road. For a short time, no one said anything, then the woman took Sylvia's hand. "Do you want to see my baby?"

The girl nodded; she would like to see the baby.

"Are you coming?" Juanita asked Larry.

Resentful at being dumped by his mother for the rest of the summer so she and his father could "work things out," Larry shook his head and looked at the ground.

"Come on," Warren said, "you'll love her." Larry looked up. Whatever Aunt Juanita meant, Larry knew she didn't have a baby, and now Uncle Warren was joining in the game. He shrugged and followed his aunt, uncle, and Sylvia around the house to the backyard.

Inside a makeshift shed with chicken-wire walls was a four-foot-tall pole with a dowel rod sticking out from it. Perched on the dowel was a small hawk. Larry couldn't believe his eyes. "A falcon!"

"A peregrine," Warren said.

The children peered through the chicken wire. On the ground lay a glove with a long leather cuff.

"The glove's so she can perch on your wrist without her talons digging into you," Juanita told them.

"Can I let it perch on my wrist?" Larry asked at the same time that Sylvia asked, "What's its name?"

"Her name's Duende," Warren said. "It's Spanish for a dark power or spirit, something like that. Larry, you can hold her tomorrow. Wait till you see her hunt. Her name sure suits her!"

That night, after the children got ready for bed, Juanita braided Sylvia's hair so she'd be cooler while she slept. She put a white sheet on the couch, and told Sylvia to lie down, then, holding one edge of a flowered sheet, she flipped it up to make it float down over the girl. Sylvia giggled and pulled the sheet away from her face to watch her aunt stuff one of the couch pillows into a flowered pillowcase. After tucking the pillow under Sylvia's head, Juanita bent down and kissed her niece's cheek.

"Is the baby lonely out there?" Sylvia asked with an anxious frown.

Juanita smiled at Sylvia's concern, "Duende's fine! Go to sleep now. Good night, sweetheart."

"Night, night," Sylvia said.

Larry's army cot on the screened-in back porch had a sheet on it too and a couch pillow covered with a pillowcase. He liked sleeping on the porch and listening to the tree frogs chirping in the yard. From the lake, not far away, came an alligator's bellow— familiar from many visits to his aunt and uncle. Drifting off to sleep, he heard a different sound, the distant tapping of a woodpecker.

He hadn't been asleep long when Sylvia tiptoed onto the back porch holding one finger to her lips as though she were shushing herself. She looked through the screen. Fireflies blinked on and off. As she pushed the door open, she glanced at her brother, half wishing he would wake up. Closing the door carefully behind her, she stepped outside.

The clouds were edged in silver; but the yard was dark and scary. She considered going back inside, but the thought of . . . what was her name?

. . . Dandy? . . . all alone gave her courage. She opened the wire gate and stepped inside. The falcon watched her. To Sylvia's surprise, the bird hissed!

"It's okay, Dandy. I won't hurt you," she whispered to the peregrine, who was moving side to side on the perch. Sylvia's eyes fell on the glove. She picked it up and shoved her hand down into it. The cuff reached to her armpit.

Duende leaned toward her.

"Don't be scared," she said in the soothing tone her mother used sometimes. She raised her gloved hand up near the peregrine's talons and kept it there, though her arm got tired. At last, Duende stepped gingerly onto Sylvia's arm. A small loop of narrow leather wound around one of its claws. The other end of the leather strip wound loosely around the end of the perch. With her free hand, Sylvia unwound that end. Distracted, she let her gloved arm fall, and Duende dropped to the ground. When she reached out for the falcon, it screeched.

Sylvia panicked and looked back at the house. No lights came on.

"Okay, Dandy, come here," she cooed. "Come on, little Dandy." The falcon didn't move.

She thought about trying to pick Dandy up and carry her; but she didn't dare risk another screech. Instead, she decided to do what she did to get Butterscotch to come out from under the bed.

"I'll be right back," she whispered and ran to the house, slipping onto the porch and into the kitchen. She opened the refrigerator door and looked for something Dandy would like. When she heard a sound behind her, she turned around. The light from the refrigerator shone on Juanita, sleepy and a little irritated; she looked from Sylvia to the fried chicken leg the little girl held in her hand.

Outside the kitchen window, Duende, trailing a leather strap, winged her way through the night.

Miles away, Mildred got out of bed. Cliff woke and reached toward her.

"I've got to go to the bathroom," she said and left the room. She was so miserable she hadn't slept a wink. Leaving the kids with her sister and Warren was Cliff's idea. She almost wished he hadn't come back home.

Cliff settled back onto the pillow to wait for Mildred to come back to bed.

A weight landed on his chest and once again he looked into the malevolent stare of the tom cat. He grabbed it by the scruff of the neck again and threw it hard. "Get out of here before I break your damn neck," he muttered.

The curtains blew inward. No rain, but Cliff's face felt wet all of a sudden. He raised his hand to his cheek. Sweat? He looked at his hand. Blood, pouring out of the gash under his eye. What the hell? "Mildred, Mildred!" he called, but no sound came out.

He put his hand to his face again. The hole was getting bigger, and so painful he thought he might black out. He pounded the bed with his fists.

"Mildred!" he called again, and again no sound came out. He grabbed his t-shirt off the floor and held it to his face. With his other hand, he felt for his jeans and yanked them on, almost losing his balance. Furious and fearful, he ran barefoot to the bathroom and opened the door, Mildred wasn't there! He ran to the kitchen. Where was she? He fumbled with the deadbolt.

"Get out! Get out!" echoed through his head.

Almost blind with panic, he didn't see Ghost, perched atop the refrigerator; but, despite his agony, he heard something. A light tapping sound made him turn. The old crone, her white hair pinned up in a feathery topknot tied with a red kerchief. She lifted her cane and pointed it at his face.

"No!" he yelled, frantically twisting the lock and yanking the door open.

His motorcycle shone in the moonlight. He leapt on—revving the engine till its roar mimicked his desperation—and rode away, a ribbon of blood streaming behind him in the night air.

On the front porch, Mildred cradled Butterscotch in her arms. "How many times do I have to call you? Let's go inside. Your kittens are hungry!" She hardly noticed the rumble of the departing past.

WATERSHEDS

STONE ANGEL

BY PATRICIA HOPPER

I am in the middle of reviewing police reports when Mrs. Burke calls and asks to discuss details surrounding her son's death. It's been only two weeks, too soon to face the grim facts. She's insistent, so I politely suggest she come down to the station. A quick intake of breath echoes over the phone like she's trying to decide if she can return to the place where she identified her only son's body. Reliving that moment can undo the delicate balance between sanity and hysteria.

"Would you rather meet somewhere else—like the Memorial Gardens?"

"It's supposed to rain," she says. "Can we meet at Mulligans Pub?"

Mulligans Pub is only a five-minute walk from Harcourt Street in Dublin, but meeting a client in such an establishment is outside my normal practice. Relating the plain facts of a life lost is no easy task anywhere; I push protocol aside and give in. Relief and gratitude flood her voice, and I'm convinced it's the right decision.

I arrive at the pub at 4:30 p.m. the appointed time, and hesitate outside the black painted exterior, large gold letters spreading the name Mulligans above the door. Wide windows face the quays along the River Liffey and a billboard sits on the sidewalk publicizing the daily menu. I take a steadying breath, push open the door, and inhale the stale smell of hops mixed with warm afternoon air. I search for her face among the half-empty mahogany tables and hardback chairs. A floorboard squeaks. I pause, then see her sitting at the bar. She looks different out of her mourning clothes. Not as fragile, not as vulnerable, almost normal. She must be in her forties, but with her light brown hair casually pulled back, she could pass for ten years younger.

She sees me and attempts a smile. "Detective Mangan. Thanks for making an exception to meet me here instead of the Garda Station…"

"No problem. It's my favorite pub."

The bartender pulls the tap drawing Guinness into a thick glass. He sets a coaster in front of me and hands me the pint. She waits till I take a sip before speaking.

"Please, tell me about my son. Exactly where did you find him?"

Details flash through my mind of vacant blue eyes, unruly brown hair, hands rolled into tight fists, a body in the fetal position, cold, unmoving. I shake loose the mental image and stick to the facts.

"We received an early morning complaint of suspicious activity in Phoenix Park. I went there to investigate. That's when I saw a male curled up beside a bush. At first, I thought it was a drunk or homeless person. Maybe he needed taken to a shelter, or the hospital. I shook him but he didn't respond. I checked his pulse. There was none. It's routine to start CPR, but there was no need. The condition of his body told me he'd been dead for over four hours. Suspecting the worst, I radioed my report into headquarters and requested the homicide unit.

"When we got to the morgue, I found a mobile phone among the victim's—pardon me—your son's personal possessions. The number for 'Mam' was listed in his contacts' directory, so I rang you. The rest you know. The homicide unit ruled out foul play, and the autopsy report stated his death was due to a heroin overdose."

I glance at her and she's weeping softly into a tissue. Ah Christ, this is what I wanted to avoid.

"Can I get you anything, Mrs. Burke?"

She shakes her head no. "Call me Sally."

She sips her Diet Coke. "I'm thankful you found him. Derek would've been glad it was you. He knew, like everyone knows, your reputation for catching drug dealing scumbags and helping kids with addictions." She hiccups and wipes away tears. "He'd been clear of drugs for over a month. He even talked about getting his life back together and going to college. For the first time since he'd started using, I began to hope. Then this…"

Laughter erupts from a table in a far corner. It sounds odd, and I want desperately to capture that carefree spirit, that happy moment, and hold onto it. I see longing in her eyes, and I know she's thinking the same.

"I must go," she says.

"Let me walk you home."

"Thanks. I don't live far."

I finish my beer, take her cardigan off the barstool, and put it around her shoulders. Outside, we walk past buildings that have long stayed the same through generations of changing patrons, changing tenants. Cars stream past, a bus screeches to a halt, somewhere a siren blares. We leave the noise behind and take a detour through church grounds, past trees green from summer rain, chirping birds, and bright red fuchsia hedges scenting the late afternoon air. Close to the church, we stop at the crucifixion scene transfixed in a stone grotto. A low iron fence surrounds it, and a kneeler invites those who want to share in Mary's sorrow.

Sally looks up at the sad face of Christ nailed to a wooden cross. A crown of thorns presses into his head and Mary's outstretched arms wait to hold her adored son. I remember the moment Sally met her own dead son. She cradled him tightly against her breast, keening the cries of a broken heart. Her lament reverberated through the cold, sterile morgue. I wanted to run from those sobs, they penetrated the very fabric of my brain.

"Mary looked on helplessly when they persecuted her son," Sally says. "Like I did. Addiction is torture. You fight it but can't win. It hounds and destroys. There's no place to turn to for help, not really. No one understands."

"There are laws to stop criminals from dealing drugs."

Her blue eyes blaze anger. "To Hell with the laws— You, of all people, know these drug-pushing lowlifes sneer at laws. They have no con-science. They're bent on destroying hearts and souls for personal gain. Money and greed are their God. They tempt the vulnerable till their minds crave only their addiction. I tried, oh, how I tried to save my Derek. I would've given my life for him. But I was no match..."

I squeeze her shoulder. We turn away from the grotto and loop back onto the busy street. We come to the cemetery gate, and she wants to go in. I hesitate. She takes my arm, and I have no choice. We walk up the avenue, sided by worn gravestones lined up in rows, one after the other.

Stone angels hover over us. She looks at one whose arms and eyes point skyward.

"Do you think Derek is one of God's angels?" she asks.

"I'm sure he is."

Her lips tremble. "Then he's found peace."

We come to a circle where paths break off in different directions. She doesn't have to look; she knows which path to take. She stops in front of a bare grave, except for a single rose and a small wooden cross bearing the name Derek Burke.

"This is his resting place. It won't look so bleak after the headstone is in place."

I already know this is her son's grave because I came to the funeral. But she was too distraught to notice me. I bend to touch the temporary wooden cross and angry bile rises in my throat. Fury battles inside me against the bastards who trapped this young man in a life of torment. I swallow my rage, and my voice sounds almost normal when I ask, "Why did you come here?"

"I want to talk to him. He knows when I'm nearby. I tell him every day how much I love and miss him."

I try to move, but my limbs are heavy. My heartbeat registers in my ears, along with something else, the shattered hearts of everyone who visits this place.

We retrace our steps on pavement laced with shadowy webs from overhanging tree branches. At the cemetery entrance, stone angels watch us rejoin the rest of the city moving forward. We come to Sally's small house, and she says, "Can I offer you a cup of tea?"

I shake my head no. "I should go." It crosses my mind she knows I haven't come just to tell her about finding her son. I'm here because I too am persecuted, and I want her to share her secret with me. How she finds the will to carry on.

She touches my arm, caressing it. For a moment, I let myself think about sinking into her arms, the lemony smell of her hair. I order myself to stop this wistful meandering before my mind stumbles into memories that will taunt me. She puts her arms around me and rests her head against my chest. Her touch, her smell, causes my knees to weaken. Something breaks loose inside me and erupts. I realize I am crying. I see it all again. Blood splattered inside our home, on the walls, on the floors, across their faces. My wife's dead body mutilated, my son's innocent body broken and beaten.

I heave long sobs, and she holds me tighter. A weight lifts from my chest and the ugly scene recedes into flickering images of my son's dark wavy hair, his boyish grin, his trusting eyes. I take his hand, and we race across the strand. My wife follows behind, her blonde hair lifting in the breeze. She yells to be careful of deceiving puddles. We stumble into a deep sandy hole. I pull my son out of the water as he begins splashing. We are soaked, but he is laughing. My wife frowns till we open our arms and welcome her in. She's soaked too, yet we are happy. So happy. This is our world, and no one can touch us...

Time stalls, and afterwards I repeat, "I should go." Sally grips me tighter before releasing me and we part without saying goodbye. I turn back toward the busy street stopping to pause again at the cemetery. I buy two roses from the tired, old woman at the flower stand. Once inside I pass the stone angels and take a different path at the circle. I find the two graves and kneel before them. Placing a rose on each one, I move my hands over the rough black ground willing them to join with the hearts that once beat.

"I arrested the drug-dealing bastards who took revenge on you to get to me," I tell my wife and son. "I swore to you I would."

I lean back on my hunkers and look out across the rows of gravestones. I beat on my chest with my knuckles. Pain shoots through me. "You got my wife and child, you lousy shites," I yell. "But you can't take away my memories—ever. They're mine. Mine..." Sucking back fury, I bury my face in the black bitter earth.

Leaving the cemetery, I pass through the church grounds and stop at the grotto. I kneel before Mary's imploring gaze. "Will my misery ever end?" I ask. "Is there no escape? For me, an arrogant fool caught up in my own self-importance, so smug in my law enforcement armor that I got my family killed. They were more precious to me than life itself. They trusted me to protect them. But I failed. Catching their bastard executioners and putting them behind bars has kept me going." I fling my hands outward, pleading. "But now that that's over what have I left to live for? I don't ask for much. Just to sleep nights."

If I expected heavenly intervention, it was obvious it wasn't going to happen. Silence lay solidly around me except for fluttering leaves, birds welcoming the closing day, and fuchsia's mellowing scent.

Outside the church grounds I re-enter the busy street crowded with people rushing home to their families, to shops, to packed restaurants, to meet friends. They hurry past, around, beside, in front of me. They are short, tall, medium, thin, round. Young and old, their hair blonde, red, black, gray, brown. Faces look happy, expectant, grim, tolerant, anxious, excited, impatient. They pulse around me like a gnawing force. Faster and faster, they move; a cranked-up kaleidoscope blurring into one muddled image. Sweat seeps through my jacket and my shirt collar cuts off air to my lungs. I can't swallow. Dizzily, I unbutton my shirt and remove my jacket. The medley of shapes begins to slow. The pace slackens. People return to themselves and continue about their business. But something's different. I begin to see, slowly at first, then more clearly, my wife and my son's likeness in each passerby.

I see my reflection in a shop window, stone-faced and motionless. I square my shoulders, heave a long sigh, and join the flow of life.

BUDAPEST LANE

By Matthew Smallwood

From where it sat on the porch railing the pitcher of tea made a hell of a filter for the surrounding valley. His was the perfect angle to peer through the amber liquid to the floating bags of Earl Gray appearing to drift above the treetops. To the way the distant cell tower's construction was now coated in the amber bronze of memorial statues and treasured keepsakes.

The elderly Russ Agel amused himself with this tea-skewed view while he lounged in his rocking chair. He scratched between Cora's ears as the two-year old German Shepherd crouched beside him. Russ checked the rope secured around her neck, to be sure the knot hadn't tightened. A terrible smell wafted off the dog and grew more pungent in the heat. Cora covered her nose with her paws and offered a single protesting whine.

"The rope's not too tight, you'll be fine. I'll take it off this evening." Russ gave the dog a gentle pat on the side. Cora looked past him to the chicken coop and the squawking birds but didn't stir from her spot in the shade.

Most of Russ's second cup was gone by the time the mailman's heavy frame came wobbling up the rocky driveway. The strain of the hike marked his postal uniform with dark sweat stains and turned his face a fiery shade of red. Porter, Russ's mail carrier of fifteen years, struggled to the oasis of the porch and deposited his colossal body on the top step.

"You know, if you had all these ruts in your driveway filled, I wouldn't have to walk across the Mohave to get here." Porter said, his words arriving as if on delay between haggard breaths. He dropped a stack of letters on the porch and joined in the ongoing vigil of the cell tower's construction. The metal monolith already reached well into the sky, sharply standing out from the otherwise rural landscape.

Porter offered a short guffaw and said, "Must be hot working on all that steel under the blazing sun. If you want my nickel's worth of an opinion, the thing's an eyesore. Like Christmas sweater ugly."

"Yep," Russ frowned as the far-off workers moved about the metal tower like scuttling insects. "They're ruining a perfect view just so people can have another bar of cell service. Some excited fella called in to the radio last night swearing those towers cause cancer. Said they grow tumors on folks like moss on an old tree."

Porter accepted the unspoken offer and helped himself to a spare cup and nearly half of what remained of the tea. He took a long drink and wiped his mouth with the back of his hand. "Who can say, maybe yes and maybe no. It should be criminal either way," Porter said with a belch. "Though, I wouldn't be surprised if half the valley doesn't end up going bald. For the rest of our lives, that's all people will see when they drive by, just one big ugly tower. Get this, they notified us at the post office that the access road going up there has been given a fancy street name. They're calling it Budapest Lane, like something out of a romance novel. Wanton lust lives on Budapest Lane. Give me a break."

Russ, a cancer survivor himself back when he still had hair to lose, put a finger to Cora's chin to feel the dog's warm breath. "Sounds classy, like a nice place to visit. Does this mean my property value will go up?"

Porter laughed, "I got a pair of binoculars in the truck. Sometimes I watch the guys working up there and it seems like there's less of them every week. The height of it must wear on a person after a while. I figure by the time they reach the top there'll be just a couple left."

Russ shifted in his chair as the sun became a slice of lemon on the pitcher's rim. "Do you really believe those conspiracy theories about cell towers making people sick?"

"Beats me, I guess anything is possible though I predict an uptick in doctor visits," Porter said with a shrug. "Hell, who really knows?"

"No one sitting on this porch," Russ replied, having experienced his own painful days of hospital visits as a young man. Visits filled with treatments he couldn't imagine undergoing in his twilight years. "Sometimes nothing makes any sense."

"Nothing here or on Budapest Lane." Porter chuckled, then fanned the air in front of his face. "What stinks? Did Cora get into the compost again?"

The dog rose at the sound of her name. She padded over for the usual pat on the head, but Porter recoiled. "Oh crap, why on Earth is there a dead chick tied around her neck? Have you lost your mind? That's animal cruelty."

Russ nodded towards the chicken coop. "I got a bunch of fresh chicks recently and Cora's been playing surrogate mom. She's obsessed with the little things like they're her pups. It'd be endearing except she's taken to carrying them around in her mouth. Poor girl doesn't realize how sharp her teeth are."

"Oh damn," Porter said. "How many has she hurt?"

Cora, not to be put out, returned to her spot by the chair and offered her belly for a scratch. Russ gave the dog a brief rub and said, "Too many. The hens have started going after her and they've stopped laying eggs. I hope smelling the dead chick all day will break her of the habit."

Porter shook his head. "There has to be a better way."

Ross stared through the nearly empty pitcher at the tall metallic spire of the tower on the other side. "If there is, no one here knows it."

BETWEEN THE LINES

By Marjorie McAtee

It's one of those ineffably clean places done in dark wood and mirrors. The bartender polishes the same glass for hours, and at this time of day I am one of two patrons. I squint toward the figure at the other end of the bar, hoping to recognize Steve or Woody hunkered down and hidden in flannel and a beaten old baseball cap. I see swatches of a wrinkled face, but nothing definite.

"Hey, old-timer," I say, moving down to sit next to him. He looks up with round, wet eyes that are yellowed in the whites. His face looks sad, deflated, like he popped it with a pin, perhaps by accident. "My name's Allen," I say when the old man doesn't respond to my greeting.

"The name's Si," the old man's voice rattles out of his lungs. "Si Hayseed."

"Hey, my granddad used to say something like that— 'My name's Si Hayseed, and I hope you know yours.'"

"Whereabouts is your granddad from, son?"

"Richwood, West Virginia."

The old man chortles, coughs, crushes out his cigarette with thick, stained fingers. His nails look hard, sharp and black. "I knew a man in Kentucky who hailed from West Virginia. Back in forty-seven, that was."

"Well hell, maybe the man you knew was my granddad. He lived a spell in Kentucky, right after he married by grandma, in nineteen forty-seven."

"What's your granddad's name, son?"

"Zeolotus Leigh."

The sagging face lengthens a little, the mouth opens like a creaky portal. "He was married to a pretty little blonde gal, wasn't he, and they had themselves a little tow-headed boy, did they not?"

"My grandma, Sarah. And they did. In E-town, I believe it was."

"Well paint me red and call me a Bolshevik," the old man chuckles. "Pleased to make your acquaintance, Allen. The name really is Si, Silas Samuel Johnson."

"Allen Michael Smith."

"Buy ya a drink, Smitty. What'll ya have?"

"Beer, pal, whatever you're drinking."

"So, how's ol' ZZ doin' these days?" Silas's eyes splash from side to side, getting drunk on my face. "Still kickin', I hope?"

"Yeah, still kickin'. You know, we expected to plant him ten years ago, but he's still pluggin' along."

"What's wrong with him?"

"Bad heart."

"Too much fried chicken, I guess," Silas says. "Damn, I ain't seen him in years. Where's he livin' now?"

"Still in West Virginia, in the same house these forty years."

"Built it himself, did he?"

"Yep."

"Sarah still with us?"

"Yep, she's in good health. Little high blood pressure, no real problems there. Broke her leg a couple years back, nothing major."

"Yeah, Sarah, she's a fighter. They both are, you know."

"Did you grow up in Kentucky?"

"Yep, I was young when I knew your granddad—fifteen years old, barely more than a kid. My father owned a general store and thought he was teaching me to run the business. He wanted me to take over when he died."

Silas stops and takes a pensive sip, stares down into the neck of his bottle.

"I guess you didn't?"

"No. I was fifteen and full of piss 'n vinegar, the way kids always are—you'll never hear me bitch about kids, I remember what it was like to be that age, I may be an old man, but I still have a good memory." Silas lights another cigarette and frowns at the smoke. "I had a fire in the seat of my pants, and I wanted to see the world. I met your granddad one day in the store, he was standing around telling war stories with the other men, joking about the French prostitutes."

The old man looks at me. "Smoke, son?" He offers the pack.

"No thanks, I don't smoke."

Silas laughs small and quiet as if this were just a bit funny. "Your granddad gave me my first cigarette. It made me sick as hell, but I smoked it anyway, because I looked up to him so much.

"They ruin your health, you know. They give you cancer."

"Yeah, I know." The old man's face darkens, but then he says, "and so does everything else." The cracked old lips stretch out, and Silas laughs again, a belly laugh that births a fit of coughing. His breath smells sour-sweet.

I rub his back, as if it were a child's back, gently. "Take it easy, old man."

"Will do, young'un."

"So, if you didn't take over the old man's store, what did you do?"

"Well truth is, son, I ran away from home, and I ain't proud of that. But your granddad said one important thing to me; he said, 'Silas, as a man in this world, you've got to take control of your own destiny. Don't let anyone else do it for you. And don't blame anyone else when things go wrong.' That was about a year after I met him, about a week before he left, and when he did, I hopped a freight to California. Mind you, this was before those faggot beatniks made a fad of it—"

"Wow, Si, that really doesn't sound like my granddad. I mean, he's really not that articulate, and besides, I would've thought he'd advise you to stay with the shop."

"He did, but I just read between the lines."

Silas stands and claps me on the shoulder with his leathery hand, farewell.

I watch him disappearing, hunched and rumpled. I order another drink, and when I try to pay, I realize he's got my wallet.

April Bird Walk Coopers Rock, West Virginia

By Elizabeth McConnell

Aged deer path in the forest.
He walks with walking stick
wearing frameless, rectangle shaped lenses
that draw you to the blue of his eye.
He is never completely clean shaven,
but close enough for you to see
wrinkles are laugh lines.
He smells of strong coffee, of juniper, of crushed leaves.
Wears a khaki ball cap with the bird club logo:
Perching Redstart.
Walking the trail, he keeps his booted feet close to the ground,
just grazing the exposed roots and ruts along the path.
But still, just so steady.
He stops when he has something to say;
Takes a thermos from his pack,
and swallows.
After so many years, he struggles for volume
but never for words.
He tells me to listen for the wood thrush
on the fallen black oak.

Pan flautist of the spring forest.
A warbler every shade of tawny,
of copper, of brass.
So hard to see among last year's leaves.
But, oh the song!

November

By Kathleen Furbee

Deep in the November woods the leaves lay thick and crisp on the ground. The autumn rains were late in coming, and a rustling nervousness rattled through the trees, trickled in the stream, drifted in the beam of a slanting sunray. *Is it coming, winter, do you know?* A squirrel skittered across the ground and ran up the trunk of an oak.

Ruth watched it run from her seat on a mossy log, the moss dry in this arid season, dry but still soft, comfortable, comforting, these small gifts, she appreciated them. She appreciated the rich loamy smell of the forest floor and the musical dribble of the stony creek. A hawk screed from high overhead and as Ruth raised her face to see it the sun reached down through the trees and caressed her face. It was a warm and gentle touch, like a sweet, sad goodbye before the ending of the day. A frosty night was predicted and, as if in preparation a sudden chilly breeze followed the sunbeam, wrapped around Ruth, and made her shiver.

Ruth scooted about on her log, adjusting her position, trying to ease the ache in her arthritic hip. Thin, fragile, and old, she had made her way down the mountain earlier in the day, leaning on her walking stick and holding tightly to the trunks of the trees. Gravity had at last been her friend. It had pulled her down the mountain, as it pulled at all living things, as it pulled and caused the breasts to sag and the back to bend and the face to droop, as it pulled and pulled life back to the earth, until life lay down and resisted no more. It was her time, Ruth knew, to resist no more.

She was proud of herself for not having fallen on her journey, and for having successfully moved her bones, unbroken, to this special place deep in the forest beside the stream. She had not been to this place in years, not since old age had slowed and made uncertain her step, but as a child and young and even middle-aged woman this had been her holy hideaway, her magical queendom. Now, it was to be the place of her final rest.

Ruth turned sideways on her log to get a better view of the creek. The stream water, partially blocked by the log, collected above it in a shallow pool. On the surface of the pool, dried leaves floated in and out of a wavering reflection of blue sky. Ruth leaned over and peered into the reflection, feeling like a witch, a sorceress, staring into a cauldron full of secrets. She saw only her own face. It was lined and loose and surrounded by white wisps of hair escaping the flowered scarf tied under her chin. She smiled at her face, at the familiar countenance which had been hers for so long, through so many years and changes. Thank you and goodbye she said, to her face, to her form. To herself, to what might be left when the form was gone, she said bon voyage.

Ruth did not consider her plan to be suicide. Suicide was active, a willful decision, and was thought by some to be a sin, an affront to a possible God, and a sure ticket to eternal hell. She didn't know if any of this was true, the sin or the God or the hell, but just in case she did not want to risk damning her soul by using pills or guns or ropes to end her life. No, in her opinion she was merely letting nature take its course. In other cultures, this graceful acceptance of nature's course was expected, and respected.

Nature had taken many courses throughout her life. Some she'd tried to stop, like the death of her daughter as a child, most she'd had to accept, like the death of her daughter as a child, and the subsequent deaths of her husband, mother, father, sisters, brothers, all of her friends. She was the last living member of her generation, at least of those known to her. At ninety-two she expected her turn was surely coming, sooner or later. She was merely removing what impediments she could in order to allow sooner to happen.

She had stopped taking her heart medicines earlier in the week. She'd mostly stopped eating several days before that. Still, she continued to wake in her bed, morning after glorious morning, to a view of sunny autumn skies and the reality of her continuing, aching, diminishing and soon to be dependent life. Her son planned to put her in a nursing home when he came in for the holidays.

The weather forecast called for steeply falling temperatures, followed by days of chilly rain. The timing was perfect- a sunny dry day for her safe descent, followed by cold and prolonged precipitation. Ruth had read up on the stages of hypothermia. First, there would be shivering, followed by disorientation, lethargy, and finally, and forever, blessed sleep. The shivering would be miserable, for Ruth did not like to be cold, but after that? Ruth pictured her body lying peacefully and still on a soft bed of leaves, deep in the heart of the forest. And her soul? She didn't know. Perhaps it would join the squirrel as it ran through the branches of the trees.

The light in the woods shifted as the sun slid behind the top of the mountain. It was time. Ruth scooted her bony bottom off the log and onto the leafy ground. The ground was soft and moist beneath the layers of leaves. Dampness seeped into the thin layer of Ruth's jersey dress. Soon it would seep into her very marrow. She lay back, resting her head against the log, beginning to shiver a little, and gazed up at the trees. They looked cold too. Cold, and naked, leafless and revealed, twisted and lumpy and bent, just like her. Unlike her, however, they were still reaching for a piece of the sky. She would not reach. She would lie, like the log, body pressed to the ground, becoming the ground, becoming the deep dark loam of the ground.

It wouldn't take long, she hoped. The hardest part had been making the decision and getting down the mountain. There was no going back now. She thought of her children, her preparations and explanations, left in a letter on her sunny kitchen table. She hoped they would understand. She had been a good woman, a good mother. She had done what she could with the life she had been given. Ruth breathed deeply and closed her eyes, beginning to shiver more vigorously. She searched her mind for final questions, doubts or fears. She had none. She relaxed her muscles against the shivering and let the cold come into her being. She breathed in slowly and deeply, taking into herself all the scents of the forest. She felt her consciousness begin to drift a little, and her body relax towards sleep.

But then, a loud crash and snort jerked Ruth from her peaceful somnolence. She opened her eyes, suddenly alert, and saw a large buck, with a huge rack of antlers and terrified eyes breathing heavily before her. Ruth sat up, hoisted by her surprise. And then she fell, squawking, as an explosion shattered her left shoulder.

"I got him Ralph!" she heard an excited male voice cry. Two men in bright orange vests ran towards Ruth as the deer leapt away.

"What the fuck?"

Ruth groaned, awake, alert, and painfully alive, as the men carried her, slung between them on an impromptu litter, up the darkening mountain.

CIGAR SMOKE

BY ADAM HORNE

Alex stared across the room, through the floor-to-ceiling windows that looked out upon the mountains. The house was built at the top of a cliff, and the room where he was now seated jutted precariously over the drop on little more than a handful of wooden beams. He yearned for his simple one-bedroom apartment, whose only window had a view of the red brick wall of the next apartment building over, just out of arm's reach across the alley.

Between him and the thin plate of glass stood a mahogany desk, behind which sat a man with buzzed gray hair and a frown. He studied Alex's face as he tapped his finger on the leather blotter. The muscles of the man's forearms rippled beneath the skin as his hand bobbed up and down. The man leaned forward and stared directly into Alex's eyes.

"Let me get this straight. You want *my permission*," and the last bit was enunciated quite deliberately, "to marry my daughter?"

Alex nodded but didn't dare speak. He'd not wanted to be here in the first place, considering this to be a rather old-fashioned custom, but Karen had insisted.

The man's eyebrows pinched together. "Why on Earth would you want to do that?"

Alex's jaw dropped open, and he replied without thinking. "Because I want to spend eternity with her."

"Eternity?" The man leaned back in his chair and laughed. "What do you know about eternity?"

Alex flinched but tried to sit up straight, despite not knowing how to reply. The laughter died off and the man leaned forward. "I had this same conversation from your side when I was about your age."

He reached into a drawer of his desk, and Alex's pulse began to race. He'd seen similar scenes in gangster movies and assumed these might be his last moments on Earth. But rather than a gun, the man retrieved a cigar box and set it on the desk. Alex let out a sigh of relief.

The man continued speaking. "Of course, my future father-in-law didn't have the giant precipice behind me to help make his point."

Alex's heart started thumping again. "Uh..."

"I'm going to ask you two questions, and I expect honest answers. If you were to fall off my balcony, how would you feel?"

"Afraid, I guess. Until I died."

"And if I let you marry my daughter? How would you feel?"

"Happy, for the rest of my life."

The man smirked. "Grab the humidor and follow me." He stood up from behind the desk and walked through a door in the glass to stand at the railing. He peered at the river at the base of the valley below them.

Reluctantly, Alex picked up the box and walked out on the landing, making sure to stay close to the wall and out of arm's reach.

"I'll give you some credit," said the man without turning. "You answered exactly how I would have when I was in the same position." He turned and scowled. "Oh, come over here. I'm not going to push you. I just wanted to make sure you were totally committed."

Alex inched forward, and the man opened the box and selected two cigars. He clipped the ends of both and put one in the corner of his mouth. Alex accepted the other when he held it out. He pulled a lighter from his pocket and held it to the end of Alex's cigar, instructing him to puff on it until the flame took hold. He lit his own cigar and returned to looking over the valley. Alex set the box on the railing beside himself.

"I hope you're right," said the man with the cigar still clenched in his teeth. "But one day you might be standing in a place like this, looking down as the water rushes over the rocks below you, and think perhaps you had the right answers but used them for the wrong questions. One day you might think back to when you were standing here and realize that only by throwing yourself over this railing would you truly be happy for the rest of your life."

Alex didn't know how to respond. Finally, he asked, "Does that mean your answer is yes?"

"Yes, you can marry my daughter."

Alex grinned, and together they looked out at the horizon as they puffed away on their cigars. After a couple minutes, the sound of knocking came from behind them.

"Is everything all right?" asked a woman's voice as the door began to swing inward.

The man quickly flicked his half-finished cigar off the balcony towards the rocks below. "Get rid of that thing!" he hissed at Alex.

Alex grabbed the stub from his mouth and hurled it to the valley floor. In his haste, he bumped the humidor, which leaned precariously then slid over the side.

"I thought you boys might like some refreshments," said Karen's mother as she crossed the office with a tray holding two iced teas and a bowl filled with pretzels. Her smile disappeared when she walked out onto the balcony. "Do I smell cigar smoke?"

The man leaned over and nudged Alex's arm as he whispered. "Tell her your news. Quick!"

"Karen and I are going to get married."

"That's wonderful!" She hurriedly set the tray on one of the wooden deck chairs and pulled him into a hug. She asked a number of questions about their plans, which he couldn't answer because they hadn't made them yet, before running inside to call her daughter.

Alex was still grinning when he turned back to find his future father-in-law staring mournfully at the ground below.

"Those were Cubans, dammit!" he lamented. "You better make my daughter really happy."

TRIBUTARIES

Heavenly Shades of Twilight Time

By George Lies

The Helvetia Blues' harmonica man holds a wavering note in tune while on stage Speedo's twelve string guitar makes old hipsters gyrate. They all unload their burdens at the Red Rose Cafe as they once did in their prime, back in the seventies.

The musical chords then take shape before twilight sets in, and seek their own freedom, skimming across flannel shirts and jeans, and lowcut blouses—weaving in close to blue collar elbowers who covet draft beers while they bounce on their bar stools.

Seeking escape, the music floats out the front door of the Red Rose Café. The notes catch a wisp of a breeze, and bounce in a rhythmic beat onto the main drag called High Street—for all of six minutes.

The harmonic pitch leaps in a spiral and bounds over low rooftops and heads downhill toward the Monongahela River where the chords flirt with leaves of water maple trees on trodden muddy banks.

The harmonic notes ride on Mon's rippled waters, turned brown by heavy rains. A crescendo tumbles onto humpbacked Holland Avenue, and whirls about a white-frame house porch, where a suntanned man holds a leather pouch he bought on a vision quest in Guatemala.

Moving toward the bridge that spans the mighty Mon, the music buzzes around a redhead girl holding a bouquet of fresh-cut roses on her way to a funeral viewing. After a solemn pause the sound wafts along the rail-to-trail path, past chipmunks hanging out with a jogger who collides with a bicyclist.

Moving on again, the music melds with the gurgles of dark brown rushing waters coming from old Decker's Creek and weaves along the boulevard, and on past the cool stream running from Cobin Creek Reservoir. The tune enjoys hovering among leafy tops of ancient oaks, elms and maples until that harmonica wail ventures creekside where a dark-haired woman reflects on water droplets leaping into a pool of life.

The music picks up a beat and glides over White Park's vacant picnic tables and worn softball fields, meandering through a forest enclave where, locals say, a real estate developer wants to cut down fruit trees to build a city golf course.

As the sun begins to sink, the mist shapes twilight time, and the rhythm reverses course. Floating over a new green playground, the rhythm first pauses in the air above a child, who is examining the cater-pillars that curl around blades of grass,

Heading toward town, the notes pass over the local graveyard where a Civil War memorial identifies a boy who faced a firing squad after he used a squirrel gun to shoot at Confederates. And nearby, a solitary fisherman is crying for he found remains of a mermaid he loved in the river—even the music pauses to admire the skeleton bones.

Crossing the High Street bridge, the music picks up speed, and criss-crosses one-way streets. The sounds halt at a dead-end alley but reverse down Pleasant Street, and goes past a barbershop, a vintage store, vacant dance hall, and an eatery once called Black Bear.

The tune escapes onto Chestnut Street and weaves by the local jail, where pigeons used to gather cooing among the rafters, until somebody poisoned them. Chords skit past the Old Stone House, built a year after that ornery Whiskey Rebellion; and bound off cobbled walls of a tavern once called Maxwells, where locals had open ears for gossip about who-did-what-to-whom.

Full circle up to the main part of downtown, the beat goes past a coffee house, an ice cream parlor, and infamous Gibbie's Pub. At a white-brick church on the steps, the sound captures pierced-ear teens who hang out mingling with brazen homeless, before they sway back on their skateboards. On the sidewalk, the harmonica pitch whirls above an agitated short bony man who is hooting out loud 'cause he holds two winning scratch-off tickets.

Squeezing over and into an alleyway, the music lingers at a CLG Radio open window and flirts with the beat of a Mexican marimba song, the notes blending as twilight begins dimming.

The music moves on, in a whirl, and stirs dust under a faded Metropolitan Theater marque. Long ago, locals bought tickets for a show by a vaudeville comedian, named Joey E. Lewis, known for a wide mouth, as well as swoon to a song-and-dance by a visiting Frenchman, Maurice Chevalier, who tipped his straw hat back in nineteen thirty-three at the end of Prohibition.

Given the fading twilight's skies, and time expiring, the music rebounds back on home. The notes resonant through the open door of the Red Rose Cafe.

The chords come to rest on the shoulder of Helvetia Blues' female vocalist, dressed in all black. She sings a new tune about change, and how she once stood on shaky grounds after her man dumped her but adds, I can see clearly now, the rain is gone. The tempo leaps in a heartbeat, back to harmonica man, who is finishing a favorite chorus, pinning down the lyrics to eve of destruction.

The music hovers around a beloved famous guitarist, Speedo by name, whose guitar zings for the old hipsters. He begs his Maybelline and asks, hey, why can't you be true. This ignites the not-a-care-in-the-world crowd to wave their arms in the air and stomp their feet on wooden planks.

At the height of ecstasy—and why can't you be true—one of the 12-strings on the guitar snaps on stage. The ricochet whacks the music man's forearm, leaving a red-flesh blemish. He lets out a common F-word. And at that moment, twilight goes to darkness.

DRAWING WHITE ASH

By Kellie Cole

Communion, the moon transparent over the house, is
etched away, the white brick looks new.

It rained and now the sun is out; it's been winter for so long
fire still warm inside the house.

The mark is light on a drawing, a white slice, the glossy edge
the absence, a blank pocket underground, a space shining
where the roof doesn't touch the wall, and light cascades over the stone.

The church may burn, dear Old Lady; a steeple crashed to cinders on the
floor
prostrated below an untouched gothic arch holding up the wall,
the cross hanging as if nothing happened before Easter.

Coloring the smoke the same charcoal smudge of the day
anything unrecoverable happens with an eraser, more graphite.

The only great face to have solace is the spring trillium, so white
the yellow center is as constant as the sun
opening time for the drawing to be complete.

TAKE ME HOME

By April Manners

Emily drove her truck into her old hometown, while her children slept peacefully in the back seat. *This place has not changed one bit. The lazy river still saunters under the old covered bridge and around the bend. The yellow caution light blinks opposite the sign that flashes cold beer. Kids still skateboard in the bank parking lot after hours, and honeysuckle still hangs heavy, perfuming the humid summer evening air. The sign outside the red brick schoolhouse announced the end of the school year and wishes for a happy summer, like when I was a kid. The old white Methodist church at the top of the hill a V shaped sign listing the times for services and a Bible verse.* A tear escaped under her sunglasses; she'd forgotten how much she loved this place.

She drove slowly across the railroad tracks, behind tractors and full wagons of fresh hay. Horses, cattle, sheep, and goats grazed in fields along the road. Emily turned off the blacktop onto a gravel road. Memories flooded back, one after another, the pond where she caught her first fish, where she and her brothers camped out. Her first horse and learning to ride, *it felt like flying.* Finally, there it was, the driveway to the big white farmhouse, with the wide front porch, the yellow porch light and the squeaking porch swing. Emily was home, but would they accept her after so much time?

George heard the thunder boom through the air, as the storm clouds rolled across the hill, the sun began its descent on the opposite hill. The wind picked up as he made it to the barn. He got off the tractor and wiped the sweat from his head with the red paisley handkerchief he kept in his hip pocket.

"Damn this rain. I was almost done," George said.

Nora turned around, "Good thing you made it back before the storm. It sounds like it'll be a gully wash."

"That it does," he said as he wrapped his arms around her. "I got all the trees planted. In a year or two they should bear fruit. And the hive house is out there ready for the bees to be added. The only thing left is to finish the berries."

"One step closer to independence and self-sufficiency," Nora kissed his cheek. "Are you ready to go to the house?"

"Yeah, let's get in there before it starts pouring."

Nora picked up the egg basket. They got into the Gator and drove to the house. Lightning lit the sky. George pulled the door open and held it for Nora, then locked it against the wind.

"Whew, that wind is ferocious," Nora said.

"What's in here?" George asked lifting the lid of the crock pot. The fragrance of garlic and spaghetti sauce filled the air as he forked a hot meatball out of the pot.

"The sauce and meatballs, get out of there. I still have to cook the pasta."

"Or I can just eat these," George said forking another meatball.

"You'll spoil your supper," Nora said pulling the garlic bread sticks from the freezer bag. "It was a stormy night like this when Emily left us."

George walked into the living room where pictures of their sons adorned the walls. Thomas and Daniel in their military uniforms, David and Seth graduating college looked down at him smiling. Their sons' wedding pictures and family portraits tacked up in honor of what they had done right. George lit the fireplace. On the mantle were pictures of their treasured daughter riding her bike with a red popsicle smile, driving the tractor, showing a cow at the county fair, and all dressed up for prom. Her leaving still cut him like a knife. "She made her choice."

⚬

Emily pulled her blue truck into the driveway, parking beside the black Mail Pouch shed where her father kept his hobby tractors, to fix up in the winter. Emily turned off the motor as she studied the farm where she'd grown up. The old red barn stood proud on the west hill. Her headlights went off as the barn's lights went off and she could see headlights coming toward the back of the house.

The wind picked up quickly, as the sky darkened to the east. *A storm is coming.* She sat quietly, listening to her children sleep, dreaming their peaceful dreams. Lights came on in the house, *they're in the kitchen. Mama probably has something in the crock pot. The whole house probably smells like the deliciousness she's created.*

Her son moved in his seat, "Are you going in Mommy?"

"Yes, baby, I want you to stay here with Gracie. I don't want her to wake up alone. I don't want her to be scared, especially with a storm coming."

"Who lives here?" Tommy asked.

"My mommy and daddy live here. This is where I grew up."

"Are we going to move here?"

"I hope so sweetheart." Emily smiled. "I'll come get you after I talk to my parents."

"Yes Ma'am," Tommy replied and saluted her.

⸺◦⸺

"I saw Wynona in town," Norma said. "She moved into a house out on Cherokee Run. She looks good. She opened a salon in town. She has really worked hard to survive after her divorce."

"Jed was a mean drunk," George said.

"I wonder if he had left with you for the Corp, if he'd have turned out different," Nora said, water glassing the day's eggs. "You know, if his dad planned the accident to guilt him into staying home."

"That thought has crossed my mind too." George picked up his fork to swipe another meatball. Thunder boomed throughout the valley, rattling the windows, followed quickly by a lightning flash. He looked out a kitchen window, sauce escaping the corner of his mouth. "Damn, that was close. I think lightning struck the old oak tree."

"We'll check it in the morning," Nora said handing him a napkin.

"Mom," The front door closed. "Are you home?"

"Emily." Nora ran to the living room. Emily stood there, in a red shirt and jeans. Her golden hair blown all around, and her hand on her swollen belly. Nora held the young woman's face, "Emily, baby, I was so worried about you. We haven't heard from you in so long. Where have you been?"

"Papa said if I left, not to bother coming back. He said Caleb was no better than the rest of his family. He said if I left, I was dead to you," Emily lowered her head.

"George, is that true?"

"Caleb's father Jed is a drunk. I've seen Wynona with more black eyes than I care to think about. Jed's grandfather has a whiskey still in the hills. I didn't want my only daughter in that mess."

"You didn't trust me," Emily said.

"It was never about trusting you. I didn't want you to throw your life away," George said.

"You thought I was throwing my life away?" Emily spat.

"I was scared of what being around Caleb and his family would make you," George said. "I'd kill him if you showed up here black and blue, or strung out on drugs, or if we were called in by the cops to identify what's left of your body."

"I told you Caleb was different. Why didn't you believe me?"

"You were so young; you saw the boy you loved. All I could see was trouble."

"Caleb hated his father's family. And do you know who he admired? You papa, you would've known that if you'd bothered to get to know him. He joined the Marine Corps, just like you. He served with honor, just like you. He was awarded a purple heart. He chose not to drink. He wouldn't even take an aspirin. We didn't just live together, we got married papa, after he got out of training, when he went to his permanent duty station," Emily said. "We've been living on base ever since."

Two small children entered the house carrying backpacks. "Mommy, Gracie woked up and was scared, so I bringed her in the house," Tommy said. Thunder boomed and the little girl screamed.

"Thank you, Tommy," Emily bent down and with a single finger she tucked the young girl's blond hair behind her ear. "It's okay Gracie; it's just a storm." Emily kissed the child on her forehead.

"Emily, you have children?" Nora asked.

"This is Tommy and Gracie, kids these are your grandparents." Emily pointed to them.

Tommy's emerald eyes looked up at his grandfather. "Pleasure to meet you sir," he said reaching out his hand.

George took the child's hand. "And you, young man."

Tommy went to his grandmother and opened his arms. "May I call you Nana?"

"That sounds perfect," Nora said hugging the child. "Where is Caleb?"

"Hey guys," Emily said to her children pulling a coloring book and box of crayons out of Gracie's backpack. "Why don't you color a picture for your grandparents, while we talk about grown up stuff?"

"Okay mommy, can we sit by the fireplace?"

"Yes, stay on the wood floor, away from the rug, in case of sparks."

Emily walked over to the other side of the living room, and spoke in little more than a whisper, "Caleb was killed overseas, getting a dozen hostages out of captivity. The mission was a success, everyone made it out, he was a hero, but he died completing his mission."

"How did he die?" George asked.

"Caleb was shot in the back, by one of the captors as he was leaving," Emily whispered so only George could hear. "He's being buried at Shady Pines Cemetery with full military honors."

"When," George asked?

"Day after tomorrow," Emily replied.

"We'll be there for you and your children," George said.

Tommy walked over to his mother, "Mommy, I'm hungry."

"Me too," Gracie said as the oven timer dinged.

"That'll be my garlic bread," Nora said going into the kitchen.

"We just ate an hour ago, you two should be fine."

"But mommy, it smells so good it's making my tummy rumble," Tommy said.

George laughed. "It makes my tummy rumble too."

"I still have to cook noodles," Nora said. "There will be plenty." Nora went into the kitchen, and they all followed her.

"Yeah," the children exclaimed.

"One more thing, we were living in base housing, but with Caleb gone I don't qualify anymore."

"I see." Nora looked at George.

"Mom you always said I could come home if I needed to, that you'd always be there for me. I know it's been a long time, but right now, my kids and I need you."

"We'll take it one day at a time," George said.

"Thanks Papa. It won't be forever. I'm a nurse, but with the baby coming and hospital shifts being 12 hours..." Emily yawned.

"Long day?" George asked.

"Yes, and I've been driving since six this morning." Emily sat down at the kitchen table as her stress and fear melted away.

"You're home now. We'll figure this out together. Tonight, you can sleep in your old room and your children can sleep in David and Daniel's room," Nora said.

"Thanks mom," Emily said. "You two hear that? Tonight, you're sleeping in your Uncle David and Uncle Daniel's bedroom. After you eat, you'll be getting a bath, jammies, brushing teeth and to bed. I will be across the hall, and your grandparents will be downstairs. No sneaking downstairs to get a snack." Emily got up and set the table.

"Supper is ready," Nora set the pot of spaghetti and sauce on the table along with the basket of bread sticks and a bowl of shredded cheese.

Emily went to the truck and grabbed their bags. With full bellies Emily and her children went upstairs for hot baths in the old claw foot tub and crawled into beds with soft blankets. They were home, safe. *Tomorrow will take care of itself*, Emily thought as she drifted off to the land of peaceful dreams.

Heart and Headwaters

By Char Tolliver

Isla Popplebrooke trekked through the thick trees, avoiding roots and low branches, but the rocky earth still made itself known through her flip flops. She fled the house so fast; they were the only shoes available. Deep within the thicket, she came to a familiar hill. Trees gave way to a ravine with a gentle rushing river below. Normally the sun would filter its rays through the trees on the other side, but the sun must've overslept on this unusually warm November day. She reached her favorite tree, its low-lying branches spread out like helping hands, and used the same branch she always did to steady herself. She paused to admire the view. Soon she would have to say goodbye to this secret piece of earth. How was she going to climb down this steep hill without breaking her neck?

Today pushed her over the edge. Months of deep breaths and yoga to combat the stress of moving, gone in an instant. The Halltons weren't her parents. They were ripping her away from her neighborhood and everything she'd ever known. Jollitown was the last connection to her real parents.

Every corner held a memory. The salon where she and her mother got their hair done, Isla's first and last perm, or the ice cream shop where they celebrated her soccer wins and consoled the losses. The hardware shop that her dad owned, where she worked her first "job." He paid her in cash and secretly threw in candy to sort all the sockets, nuts and bolts. Her heart broke to see it sold to a conglomerate. Then there was *that* corner, the one she walks a half a mile out of the way to avoid. It's earmarked by

Tripp's Tavern, a stone's throw from the movie theater her parents were walking to when a drunk driver swerved then overcorrected. The grill of his truck marred their bodies so badly, she didn't even get to see them. No goodbyes, just suddenly a whole new life with the Halltons, Mark and Tessa, her godparents.

Four years she lived with the Hallton clan. Why did she have to move with them? Why couldn't she finish her year here and graduate with all the people she'd ever known? Or pick her own college? Just because her adoptive family was paying her tuition didn't mean she had no say. The "my house my rules," order wore as thin as an old shirt washed so many times it gave way to holes. Bad enough they had to move, but now she had to reapply to colleges and fast. Submissions were closing soon, if they hadn't already.

A jagged rock sunk into her flip flop, hurting her foot. She ripped the rock that stabbed her foot from the dirt. Smooth on the bottom. Of course that wasn't the side her foot found. She hurled it into the water and watched the ripples move outward. At least her actions influenced something, if only for a moment.

Sitting on a semi-flat patch of grass, a ways down the hill, she drew her knees to her chest and squeezed her throbbing foot. A breeze tore through the ravine, whipping through her shoulder length hair, taking her pain with it. It should relocate her to another family too. Preferably one staying here.

Grow up. Get a job. Buy a house. Blah. The idea of spending years reliving the same day over and over until something - anything - intervened to change the course was maddening. How long would the water have stayed calm if she hadn't thrown the rock in? Isla didn't want change to happen to her, so wanted to *be* that change, forging her own destiny. Community colleges had exactly zero appeal. If she caved, what next? Would her adoptive parents force her to follow their path of education? Great path, but not for her.

Footsteps crunched behind her. No one knew this spot existed. Well, the few who did never bothered to make the hazardous climb down. Most people would freeze in fear. Isla wasn't 'most people.' Boring.'

The steps grew closer. "Taking the sister duty seriously, huh, Stella? Really, I'll be fine," she said without looking up. Isla withheld the laugh begging to escape when she heard the stumble down the hill.

"Thought I'd find you here," a warm, familiar voice said.

She whipped around, no longer able to withhold her smile. "Landon. I didn't expect you." He climbed down to her with his arms out to the sides, wobbling but refusing to fall. "You're seriously trying to surf down the hill?"

"Hey, it's working." He let out a dramatic yelp. "Is this what they mean when they say you're falling for someone?" He laughed but continued to stare at the hill.

"Funny." Small rocks rolled into her thigh shortly before he stopped next to her. He sat down beside her, pulling off a backpack. "Figured you might want these." He handed her socks and hiking boots.

"Hey, how'd you...Stella."

"Yeah, she texted me."

"What did she tell you?" Isla put on the socks and squeezed into the boots. They felt so much better.

"Just that you needed a friend and maybe a good pair of boots." He tucked her flip flops into the bag then put his arm around her. "You know you can tell me anything, right? I mean, we're best *friends...*" he trailed off. He always highlighted the word *friends*. His presence here and his arm around her...could he be indirectly telling her that their friendship meant something special to him? If only he'd be clearer about his feelings, maybe she could admit that she thought about him as more than a friend too.

"We're moving to Ohio..." She hesitated, giving him a moment to respond and he nodded. "Mark got a job so we're leaving sooner than expected. I don't get to finish school here. It's like finalization of the adoption took my voice away. They've always pushed community college, but now I have no choice. It's Clark State. I'm *not* a Hallton. I don't want a pre-planned, mediocre community college life like they have. The next thing I know, they'll tell me what to major in, and who to marry." She blushed and lowered her eyes, when she realized what she said. Must be the influence of his musky cologne.

She curled into his side to hide her tears. "I'm sorry," she whispered. He didn't answer, instead he wrapped his other arm around her and rested his head on top of hers.

"I remember the first day I met you in school," he said. "You looked smart. When I asked you to tutor me in science, I didn't expect you to say no." He let out a chuckle. "You never told me why. I know you aced Mr. Mathis's class. So why not?"

Even knowing she'd never see him again; no rush of courage came. Spilling her guts would be like opening a door to slam it on her fingers. It's high school. No one ends up with their high school sweetheart, right? Silence stretched while Isla considered his question before speaking. Moving in with the Halltons meant going to the other middle school. No one reaches out to the new girl the first week of school unless it's some form of taunting. Every movie depicts the new kid as either a troublemaker or a wallflower. She was neither and didn't fit any category. Not a jock, goth, nerd, popular...and she didn't want to live by a set of invisible rules. Those groups all came with some unspoken code.

"Why ask now, after all these years?"

"Humor me." He shrugged but didn't remove his arms.

Isla was afraid if she spoke, his embrace would end. The wind still ran its fingers through her hair, but instead of wishing it to whisk her away, she now wished for it to stand still, in this moment forever...as long as she didn't have to answer.

The warmth of his embrace set all the butterflies in her stomach aflutter. She pulled back and looked him in the eye. "Why ask a new girl for help?"

Landon's gray-blue eyes locked with hers. The wind ran its fingers through his thick, dirty blonde hair. What a beautiful man. That thought never changed in all the years they've known each other. With him so close, all her nerve-endings exploded, and her brain couldn't hold a single thought. Empty. All she could focus on was him.

The wind died down and he whispered, "Like I said, you looked smart, and I know you aced Mr. Mathis's class,"

"You know I'm moving, and I'll never see you again." She blinked back silent tears threatening to stream down her face. Why was it so hard to simply say she had feelings, and leave interpretation up to him?

"When are you moving?"

"Before Christmas."

"What are you going to do about college?" He pushed a stray lock of hair behind her ear.

"I don't know. Looks like I'll go to Clark State, if I go at all."

"You should go, but in exchange, you choose your major."

With his fingers slowly making their way through her hair, she wanted to shush him. "I don't want to talk about college."

"Isla, why didn't you tutor me?" he whispered, gently lifting her chin so they were face to face.

Answering him honestly felt like baring her soul. She closed her eyes and drew a deep breath. "You were kind, and you noticed me. It was shortly after everything that happened with my parents. Moving in with the Halltons meant going to the Junior high where I didn't know any-one, but they all knew of me. Nobody ever asked me what I wanted. But you saw and I couldn't believe it. I panicked. And you were gorgeous with those eyes, and I couldn't believe you would be interested in me. I had to stay away if I was going to keep from falling...How could I tutor you one-on-one?"

Landon absorbed her answer, then moved in, putting his lips to hers, gentle but full of passion. Sparks...the fourth of July had nothing on the display her stomach put on. He pulled back and put his forehead to hers. "Man, I've wanted to do that for a long time. I needed to be sure..."

"But..." Their kiss encompassed everything from hello to goodbye. "I'll never see you again." She couldn't stop the tears streaming down her face. "What'll happen between us? Long distance doesn't work." Her gaze fell at her own words. This was the inevitable door slamming on her fingers. Maybe her heart.

He reached inside his bag, rummaging for something. He put an opened letter addressed to him in her hands. "Open it."

"I don't understand." She raised an eyebrow at him.

"Read it," his voice was laced with excitement.

She opened the letter. "Congratulations...you've been accepted to Clark State College..." She looked up at him. "Is this for real? But how?" She squealed.

"I applied to Clark College after you first hinted you may have to move and go to a community college... and to every other college in the area, just in case. I was working up the courage to tell you, but I didn't know how. Your tutor rejection weighed on me over the years. I thought I'd have to accept being friends forever." He intertwined his fingers with hers. "I don't want us to end."

"You would do that for me?"

"Yes, and a lot more if you'll be my girlfriend." Landon pulled her in for a second kiss. He nibbled on her lower lip and moaned when she returned the favor.

"I thought you'd never ask," she said when he released her.

"I love you. I can finally say it." He leaned and kissed her again.

THE STYLUS OF TAMERLANE

BY MATTHEW SMALLWOOD

Joseph Walker departed his home on the morning of October the third in a dismal and exhausted state of flummoxing turpitude. His nighttime coupling with the coverlets and eiderdowns had bequeathed no recompense nor respite from the previous twelve-hour day at the press. There had been no blissful trip to the lands of Nod. No merriment, in the memories or indulgent fantasies of the buxom and wanting.

For the devil's own reasons, the witching hour had entailed a torment of lucid hallucinations presenting the false flag of dreams. From the first moments, where he had gazed upon the smoldering skies of ash, Joseph had known it to be a nightmare. The black smoke of the heavens aflame obfuscated the roads and Baltimore had become the city of fire.

Purged and removed from God's Earth, Joseph awoke in a heap, half-strangled by the bed sheets and his own clawing fingers. He stifled the scream, but not the terror which removed further sleep and caused a fitful pacing as though waiting on the arrival of a late-night visitor.

The dawn came and with the banishment of night. Wednesday, gowned in frost, marched midway across 1849.

Joseph put boots to the road and drudged into the cold of Lily-Liver Street on his way to the shop. Vagabonds used the backways for their drunken jaunts between the pubs and parishes, so their placement had become landmarks on his daily trek.

Ryan's Tavern was closing-up in observance of the fishery's sobering shift whistle. The inebriated and downtrodden shuffled out like suited cards spread across a dealer's table. In the chill, one oddly dressed beggar lurched as if the spirits had taken control of his brain.

Today, charity and goodwill were not the tallest spires in the mansion of Joseph's temperament. He shuddered in a salty, sharp, breeze and said, "You'll get nothing from me today ragman, now shove off."

The beggar hitched on the uneven cobblestones in clothes too large for his small stature. On his head was martyr thin hair cut from dark quartz and gravestone. The beggar exhaled a whispering like a sea spray off the tide and put vacant, bloodshot eyes on Joseph's.

"Reynold's, Reynolds," the bum moaned before fainting into the gutter.

Joseph thought something in the haggard face hinted at a previous meeting. Under other circumstances they had indeed crossed paths before, except the fainting fellow had been no derelict then.

"Mr. Poe? Edgar," Joseph said, joining the author on the cold street. "Mr. Poe, its Joseph, the printer. I'll find a doctor. You just remain still."

"Reynolds, whiskey, Snodgrass, the Doctor J. Snodgrass, address him of my constitution," Mr. Poe whispered, a feverish muttering perforated by droplets of crimson spittle.

A meandering group of gossiping magpies arrived and soon thereafter a stretcher to carry the ailing poet to the hospital. The gathered magpies in the guise of curious citizens hurled barbed and serrated squawks of gossip at those attempting to lend aid.

"That's the drunk who wrote that awful story about The Cigar girl," one said.

"He married his cousin you know. He'll shoulder the Lord's wrath for such a beastly act."

"I heard he killed her," another one remarked in the mewling tone shared by every woe monger.

On the stretcher the writer said one final thing, and Joseph was close enough to hear. "God, judge not my spirit as Erebus coal. Lord be with mercy. Mercy, Lord help my poor soul."

Washington College Hospital took in the author, Edgar Allan Poe, and sequestered him away in a private room. Joseph, bearing a rescuers' concern for the harsh malady he had witnessed firsthand, sought to bring the poor man comfort. The Physicians however, refused to allow any visitors and cited a bedside delirium of paranoid fear in Mr. Poe's fractured psyche.

Sunday, October Seventh, 1849.

Edgar Allan Poe passed away into the night.

MORGANTOWN WRITERS PROFILES

Jeremy Bock is a West Virginia native and technologist currently expatting in Bangkok with his wife and daughter. His novel, Caroline, is independently published and available on Amazon. Short stories are available for browsing on social media: X @jbockcet, Instagram @jbockwrites and on Facebook. (facebook.com/jbockwrites).

Eric Casdorph was born and raised in Morgantown, West Virginia. He graduated West Virginia University in 2020 with a degree in English. He has previously been published in Everyday Fiction, and spends most days writing, cooking, and learning how to be a better person than he was the evening before.

Kellie Cole is a licensed architect practicing in West Virginia who teaches architecture at Fairmont State University. She joined the MWG in February of 2024. Kellie's poetry has been published in Whetstone, Fairmont State University's publication, and Voices From the Attic.

Justin Crawford spent his childhood wandering through forests, daydreaming, and writing. He completed a Master of Fine Arts in Creative Writing from West Virginia University in 2012. He currently lives in Bridgeport, West Virginia, with his wife, two children, two cats, one dog, and a tortoise named Sir Terry.

Jane Ellen Freeman's recent stories appeared in the following: Vol. V of the Northern Appalachia Review, Vol. XVI of the Anthology of Appalachian Writers, The Ghosts of Shepherdstown Vol. I. Her story "Connection" will appear in Vol. XVII of AAW. Published books can be found at www.janeellenfreeman.com.

Geoffrey C. Fuller work has appeared in 21 books, among them a crime fiction novel, Full Bone Moon, and the New York Times bestseller, The Savage Murder of Skylar Neese. His latest nonfiction, The WVU Coed Murders, accompanies a podcast about the case. "Bucket of Blood" grew out of the research for that book.

Kathleen Furbee writes short and long fiction, poetry, and creative non-fiction. Her work has been published in several anthologies and literary magazines including Anthology of Appalachian Writers, Appalachee Review, Kestrel, and others. She was a former member of the Morgantown Writers Group and participated in several Goldenrod workshops.

Aimee Hoffer grew up in Wheeling, WV. She started writing poems and stories in grade school and won her first poetry contest in middle school. She moved to Morgantown, WV in 2007 and joined the Morgantown Writers' Group shortly after. She is currently at work on a novel.

Patricia Hopper Patteson a native of Dublin, Ireland, resides in West Virginia. She holds a B.A. and M.A. from West Virginia University (WVU). Her fiction and non-fiction have been published in magazines, newspapers, reviews, and anthologies. She is the author of an Irish historical trilogy, romance, and romance-suspense novels.

Adam Horne writes in the fantasy and science fiction genres. He has five books published on Amazon, including his LitRPG series Genesis Online. He is currently developing a fantasy series based on Japanese mythology. Visit www.authoradamhorne.com for news and other information about his novels.

Brian Scott Horne is an occasional scientist and amateur writer. He studied Biology and English at West Virginia University and holds a Master of Science degree in Biological Sciences from the University of California, Irvine. He enjoys reading scientific research journals and helping others incorporate real world science into their stories.

Cerid Jones is a life-long closeted writer learning how to be brave with sharing her musings. A lover of folk tales and myth, hailing from Aotearoa (New Zealand). Growing up in a house with more books than wall space and fae at the bottom of the garden, she's always been a creature with a passion for arts and literature. Reading anything transporting her elsewhere or delving into the psyche of human nature, she works in publishing and sometimes teaches axe-throwing. Published in WildRoof Journal and Viewless Wings, her Instagram is @curiouscerid.

Norman Julian is the author of five books, thousands of news stories, columns, features and editorials. He is founding editor of Panorama magazine. He owned Trillium Publishing, now with new owners. George Lies was a long-time friend, mentor, and counselor.

Ethan Andrew Kelley is a short fiction writer born and raised in West Virginia. He writes science fiction and horror. Outside of writing, he works at West Virginia University as an analyst. He enjoys spending time with friends and family, attending Jiu-jitsu classes, and acting in small film and TV roles around Pittsburgh.

Jenna Lapointe has degrees in psychology and creative writing from Washington College and enjoys writing both short and long form contemporary fiction with a focus on mental health and a flare of surrealism. She currently works remotely while traveling with her miniature Australian shepherd, Wade.

Lore Lee is a social worker who provides guidance on the Americans with Disabilities Act by day and writes experimental fiction, sci-fi, and character-driven stories by night. They enjoy jogging and reading in their spare time and would love to travel somewhere with plenty of crickets and no light pollution.

George Lies was the founder of MWG. Recent publications are: Trolling the Reservoir at Short Fiction Break and Hollywood Audition Call at Reedsy, UK. He was on Morgantown Sister Cities Commission working with Guanajuato MX and Xuzhou CN; and was on the board of WV Council of International Programs. In September. 2019, the well-known Mexican Poet Benjamin Valdivia, hosted him for a reading of La Galeria (in Spanish) at Guanajuato University.

April Manners was born in the Appalachian Mountains. She is the daughter of a Vietnam Veteran and learned about patriotism at home. Her coal miner and farmer grandparents taught her about work. She tried to escape Appalachia, graduating from college in Massachusetts, before her mountain roots called her back home.

Marjorie McAtee writes poetry and nonfiction. Her work has also appeared in Flashquake, Center: A Journal of the Literary Arts, and Amarillo Bay, among other publications. She lives in Wheeling, WV with her husband and their children, who are cats.

Elizabeth McConnell earned a BA in English, concentrating in Creative Writing, from Hollins University. Elizabeth is a member of the Morgantown Writers Group, Monongahela Master Naturalists, and WV Writers, Inc. She enjoys writing Natural History essays as well as poetry rooted in Nature. Her work has recently been published in One Art, Voices From the Attic and The Northern Appalachia Review.

S. James McLaughlin is co-producer of the podcast, *Appalachian Mysteria,* and hosts other true-crime podcasts. She is also co-author of *The WVU Coed Murders: Who Killed Mared and Karen?* As a child, Sarah was often left unattended at her grandparents. There she discovered her grandma's true-crime gore-porn stash. The rest is history.

Tom Musbach joined the Morgantown Writers Group in 2022. His creative writing appears in a few LGBT anthologies, and he's currently working on a novel. He holds an MFA in Creative Writing from the University of San Francisco.

Andrei Nesteroy (Андрей Нестеров) is a WVU graduate from Russia. He works in cross-cultural communication between American and Russian scholars and students. His focus is on exploring the culture of both the countries and writing stories about different cultures and lifestyles.

Alan O'Conner needed a challenge so as not to fail retirement. Two creative writing courses later, he joined the MWG. Through George Lies leadership and supportive peer learning, Alan evolved into a writer of action-adventure stories. He lives now in Boise with his wife Karen.

Bryce Painter is a writer of science fiction, fantasy, and poetry from southern West Virginia. He is currently in the process of writing his first novel and earning a Master of Fine Arts degree in creative writing.

Edwina Pendarvis lives in Huntington, WV, and is retired from Marshall University. Among her publications are dual-language biographies published by Shanghai University Press; poetry collections, including Ghost Dance Poems; and her most recent book, Another World: Ballet Lessons from Appalachia. She's book review editor for Pine Mountain Sand & Gravel.

Janis-Rozena Peri received the Bachelor of Music in Piano from Otterbein and the Master of Music in Voice from Miami University. Her debut recital at Carnegie Recital Hall received rave reviews in The New York Times. Ms. Peri was appointed to the voice faculty of Old

Dominion University, and later to the voice faculty of West Virginia University.

Alexandra Persad received a Bachelor's degree in English from West Virginia University. She now lives happily in Michigan with her partner and cat, Jasper. She continues to pursue creative writing and has published work in various online journals. In 2023, her fiction was nominated for a Pushcart Prize.

Stan Pisle is a Berkeley California poet and writer with roots in rural communities in West Virginia, Kansas, and Idaho/Montana. His works have appeared in literary journals, magazines, the occasional textbook, on NPR, and radio stations in Montana.

Laura Rayburn has spent most of her life in West Virginia. She has a bachelor's in creative writing and a Master's in education. She currently teaches in the Morgantown area. She loves plants, animals, reading, playing video games, and spending time with family.

Melissa Reynolds has a Masters of Professional Writing and Editing and is an editor with The Metaworker Literary magazine, a NYC Midnight judge, and a freelance editor. She lives in Morgantown, West Virginia with her four children. She has published several stories and poems at various magazines and in her spare time rescues discounted plants.

Matthew Smallwood was born and raised in West Virginia. He's had numerous short stories published in various anthologies and his debut horror novel Immortal Again is available on Amazon.

Emily Stanton is an engineer/writer obsessed with exploring ideas through sci-fi and fantasy. She is a WV native and an incoming freshman at California Institute of Technology, where she will study Mechanical Engineering. Emily has been part of the Morgantown Writer's group throughout high school and thanks them for their support in her writing journey.

Char Tolliver ADD kept her spinning until one day she had surgery and recovery forced her to be still. The stories that swirled in her mind forced their way out and her love of writing intense stories across different genres was born. Since then, she's switched careers, moved across the big city of Indianapolis, and had 2 kids. Life's still spinning, writing simply joined the circle.

Gwenyth Winship is an emerging writer from New Hampshire. She has a B.A. in history from Brown University. She is a D1 Women's Track & Field medalist, who moved to West Virginia in 2022 to work for the U.S. Department of Justice. An active member of the Morgantown Writer's Group, she also enjoys exploring the Appalachian history and the outdoors.